Di ISLAND CREW INVESTIGATES

The
CASE
of the
HAUNTED
WARDROBE

Kereen Getten

Illustrated by Leah Jacobs-Gordon

Pushkin Children's

Pushkin Press
Somerset House, Strand
London WC2R 1LA

The Case of the Haunted Wardrobe was first published by Pushkin Press in 2023

1 3 5 7 9 8 6 4 2

ISBN 13: 978-1-78269-392-5

Designed and typeset by Tetragon, London
Printed and bound in the United Kingdom by Clays Ltd, Elcograf S.p.A.

www.pushkinpress.com

KIRSEN (?)EN grew up in Jamaica, where she would climb fruit trees in the family garden and eat as much mango, guinep and pear as she could without being caught. She now lives in Birmingham with her family and writes stories about her childhood experiences. Her work has been shortlisted for the Waterstones Children's Book Prize, the Spark Award, the Warwickshire Junior Book Award and the Diverse Children's & YA Prize. Her first book is the LH Island Crew: Investigator Keita. The Tale of the Lighthouse Fiends ... Mischievous Book of the Island? When We Chase the Monsters and/ You Fool Our ... ... from Pushkin Children.

The CASE of the HAUNTED WARDROBE

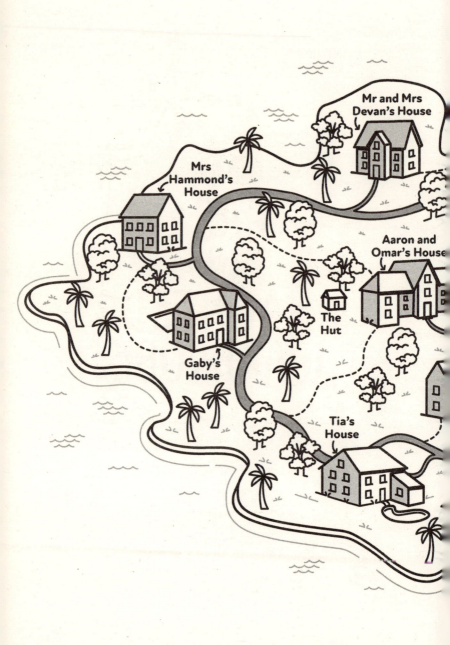

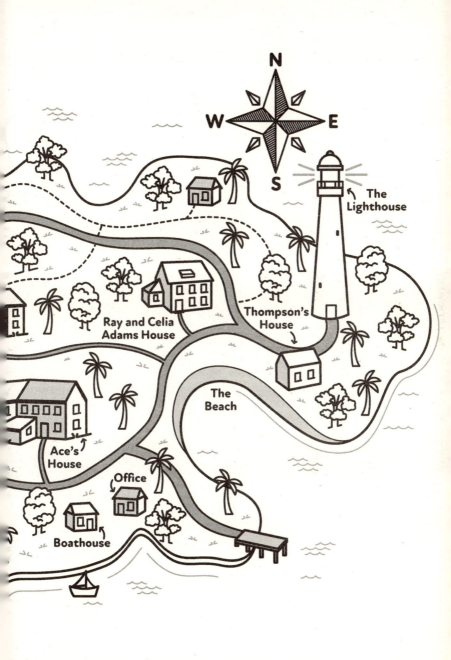

The Lighthouse

Thompson's House

Ray and Celia Adams House

Ace's House

The Beach

Office

Boathouse

Chapter 1

Yo, we're going to the island for winter break, my cousin Aaron texted me last week. *Mum wants to know if you're coming?*

Of course I'm coming! I replied almost immediately.

Going back to Lighthouse Island is all I've been thinking about since I was there last school break. I miss the small island, with its quiet cove and towering lighthouse that doesn't work. I miss the hut at the end of my cousins' garden, where we meet with the rest of the gang. I miss Elma the housekeeper making delicious treats, and I miss Di Island Crew, our detective gang. Most of all I miss Gaby. She's the one person who made me feel at home on the island, who became my best friend.

Mama has lost her temper with me a few times since Aaron texted, because I can't concentrate on anything else.

"Fayson, I don't want to hear about no island adventure until you finish your homework," she said last time I brought it up. "I'm sick of hearing about 'Island this and island that'."

I fell silent, not wanting to upset her any more, but continued to doodle on my notepad:

Island Adventures, Here I Come!

Now the day has arrived, I am filled with excitement to see the island and my friends.

I have waited all morning for my cousins to pick me up, jumping up every time I think I hear a car pull into our car park. Finally they arrive early afternoon, just as Mama and I are sitting down for lunch.

I hear a car horn and jump up from the table, running to the window with a half-eaten corned-beef sandwich in my hand.

"Fayson, finish your lunch," Mum orders.

I peer out and my heart skips a beat.

"They're here, Mama!" I cry, stuffing the rest of the sandwich in my mouth.

Mama glares at me. "Finish your lunch."

I turn to her, exasperated. "But they'll be waiting for me."

Mama takes a sip of her sorrel tea. "Waiting won't kill them," she says. "Sit."

I reluctantly pull myself away from the window and slump into the hard chair. I try to stuff the last two sandwiches in my mouth as quickly as I can.

"Fayson, eat it properly," she snaps.

There is a knock on the door, and I look to Mama. She gets up from the table and walks over to the front door. She opens it and I see Uncle Edmond and Aaron outside.

Mama and Uncle Edmond greet each other with an awkward nod of their heads.

"She's still eating lunch," Mama says.

I stuff the last piece of sandwich in my mouth and jump to my feet. "Finished!"

Mama shakes her head. "Go and freshen up."

I groan, push back the chair and rush to the bathroom down the hall.

When I return, Uncle Edmond and Aaron are standing in the living room.

"You've done this place up nice," Uncle Edmond says, looking around.

Mama is in the kitchen pouring two glasses of water. She brings them through. "I do what I can," she replies.

Aaron and Uncle Edmond drink their water in silence.

I grab my bag as I enter the living room. "Ready," I announce, desperate to get Aaron and Uncle Edmond out of our tiny apartment, and away from the heavy silence.

Uncle Edmond gives me a small smile. "Good," he says with a nod. "Shall we go?"

Outside the apartment, Aaron and I walk ahead of the adults, who follow us without speaking. Uncle Edmond makes a half-hearted attempt at a conversation, but Mama barely offers an answer.

"I like your place," Aaron says as we head down the steps that lead to the car park. "It's cosy."

It's been a few years since Uncle Edmond or the twins have been to our home. The last time they came, Omar announced that our apartment was the same size as his bathroom and bedroom put together, then proceeded to run through the apartment to make sure.

I narrow my eyes at Aaron.

He throws his hands up in the air. "What? Cosy is good."

I shake my head. "Just say it's small," I tell him, as we walk across the car park to their familiar black SUV.

"Nope," Aaron says. "I'm sticking with cosy."

Uncle Edmond takes my small bag from me and puts it in the boot of the car. My cousin Omar—Aaron's twin—sits inside with Aunty Desiree, Uncle Edmond's wife.

I hug Mama tightly.

"Be good," she whispers in my ear. "Listen to your uncle and don't cause any trouble." She holds me at a distance, looking me over as if checking I am dressed and lotioned. "I don't want stories coming back to me about your behaviour," she says, running her palm across my face.

I nod firmly. "I won't let you down, Mama." I let go of her and slide into the open door of the car. Omar acknowledges me with a fist bump.

"Welcome, weirdo," he says.

I beam with excitement, refusing to let him ruin this day.

"How was school?" Aunty Desiree asks, as I climb in. "Did you do well this term?"

"Yes, I did well, Aunty," I tell her, even though I have been told off at least three times during school term for daydreaming in class. Aunty Desiree can be so serious about school. Much more serious than Mama.

I roll the window down and wave to Mama, who's standing in the car park of our apartment block, her arms folded against her chest. Barry, my annoying neighbour who goes to the same school as me, watches from his balcony.

"Dat car too nice for you," he shouts down at me through his cupped hands. Mama turns to look up at him. Barry flashes her

an innocent smile. "Ms Mayor, what a pretty dress yuh wearing."

Mama shakes her head, turning back to me just in time to catch me sticking my tongue out at Barry. I sink back into the car seat as she approaches, expecting her to tell me off. She leans into the car window and kisses me on the cheek.

"Stop being so rude," she says, before stepping back.

Uncle Edmond gets into the front seat, closing his door and winding the window down. "You sure you don't want to come?" he asks Mama.

She shakes her head, folding her arms again. "That life is not for me." She glances at me, then shifts from one foot to the other. "But I'll never say never," Mama adds. "Fayson seems to enjoy it, so it can't be too bad over there."

My eyes widen. Did Mama just say something nice about Lighthouse Island?

"Well, when you're ready," Uncle Edmond says. "There's always a room for you."

Mama doesn't reply, just gives him a short nod.

Uncle Edmond rolls his window up, locking the tension inside. He and Aunty Desiree exchange a look between them, and I sink even further into my seat.

During the journey to the boat, I think only of Mama: what she must be feeling now I have gone, and how she is alone in the apartment without me.

The sun has not come out once today. When we reach the boat that will take us to the island, the sea is particularly rough, a sure sign it is about to rain.

As we climb on to the boat, Uncle Edmond shouts, "Is there a storm coming?", to no one in particular, and the boat captain responds.

"Yep, we're in for a bumpy ride. Rougher than normal," he says, squinting out to sea. "Might be coming sooner than we think."

"Well, I hope it's after we reach shore," Uncle Edmond replies.

I clutch my bag to my chest and close my eyes tightly, hoping that we make it to the island before any storm. It would be terrible if we all got swept away and I drowned and never saw Mama again. I feel sick suddenly at the thought. Or maybe my sickness is due to the boat setting off, bouncing over the choppy water.

I grab on to the seat with one hand, gripping my bag with the other. I feel every bump of the waves. The spray of the sea on my face. I try to drown out the roar of the ocean each time we meet a swell, gritting my teeth and silently begging it to be over.

Chapter 2

Luckily, we make it to the island before any rain, and I am relieved to get off the boat.

As we all step on to the jetty there is a screech of excitement, and Gaby comes running towards us. Ace is strolling behind her.

I drop my bag and run towards Gaby, who I met here on my last visit. Of everyone I met in the group on the island—Aaron, Omar, Tia, Gaby and Ace—she was the one who made me feel the most welcome. We meet in the middle, clashing against each other, arms entangled, voices squealing, jumping around in circles until we are out of breath.

Gaby and I have grown close on the mainland. We talk every day on the phone; about school, and about parents and how they don't understand us. But most of all we talk about the island and all the adventures we are going to have.

I have shared secrets with Gaby that I have never told anyone else, because I trust her. She is the best friend I've ever had. One day I hope I'll trust her enough to invite her to my apartment. I will show her all my books, and we'll read together and go to the beach, maybe even have ice cream—just like I did with my best friend Lizzy before she moved away.

Lizzy used to be my best friend. My only friend. We liked the same things and did everything together. We would read our favourite books in the living room, with the door open while Mama hung the washing out, the soft morning breeze giving us some relief from the rising sun. After lunch we would sit on the balcony, our legs hanging over the side, pretending we were royalty and all the people below were our subjects. Lizzy understood me. She never laughed at me for loving books and never made fun of me for the games I wanted to play. She was my favourite person in the whole wide world. Then, one day, she was gone.

I link arms with Gaby, following Aunty Desiree and Uncle Edmond over to their golf carts.

"I've been counting the days on the calendar until we saw each other," I tell Gaby.

She squeezes my arm. "Me too. I wonder what adventures we'll have this time?"

As if on cue, the sound of thunder explodes in the sky, and the heavens open. We run for the shelter of the buggy, screaming as the rain soaks us to the skin.

Uncle Edmond tuts as we jump on to the back of the buggy. "It's only rain. No one's going to die!"

We drive up the hill, the wind sweeping sheets of rain inside the buggy. I can see Tia's house from here. I catch a glimpse of her bedroom window, where she said she could watch over the island. Tia and I never got along on my last visit. She was the leader of the group and didn't particularly like the twins bringing me to the island. We clashed almost every day, and when I left the island last summer, she wasn't talking to any of us.

I'm almost sure I see a shadow in the window looking out, but the rain is so thick that I can't tell if it's Tia or the shadow of the trees.

Uncle Edmond parks the buggy right outside their front door, and Aaron—who was allowed to drive the second buggy—parks behind us.

Gaby grabs my hand and rushes from the buggy to the front door, just as Elma opens it to let us in.

Inside Uncle Edmond's house, Elma hugs me tightly even though I'm soaking wet.

"It's so good to see you, Ms Fayson," she says, letting me go and handing us all towels that were hanging over her shoulder. We dry ourselves off as best we can while Aunty Desiree moans at us to stop dirtying the floor.

I grab Gaby's hand and rush through the house. The smell of Elma's banana bread fills every room.

The sound of Uncle Edmond's heavy feet echoes down the hall to his office. He shouts that he doesn't want to be disturbed unless someone is dying.

"Take those wet clothes off and put them in the laundry room!" Aunty Desiree shouts after us.

We run into the kitchen and steal slices of banana cake. It's so warm it melts in our mouths! "It's not ready yet!" Elma cries, catching us. We run out, giggling.

I notice the dark, cloudy sky through the large floor-to-ceiling glass doors and the skylight. Every time we pass a window, the sound of the rain pounds against the glass like a demon trying to get in.

We reach my room, which is on the left of the long bedroom corridor. I run in, throwing myself on the bed and snuggling into the freshly washed sheets. Gaby jumps next to me, narrowly missing my head, which only sends us into screeching laughter.

We turn to each other and scream, "I missed you," at the same time, wrapping our arms and legs around each other like an octopus.

"This weather sucks," Omar mumbles, entering my room and heading over to the glass doors. He stares out at the thick sheet of rain, with his hands in his pocket like an old man. Aaron and Ace follow a little way behind, talking in lowered voices.

"What are you two whispering about?"

I ask curiously, sitting up. Aaron shrugs his shoulders. "We were wondering what the plans were for the gang."

I climb off the bed and reach for my bag, pulling out a large folder. "I've thought about all that," I tell them proudly. "I have some ideas, if you want to hear them?"

"Of course we do," Gaby says, looking over my shoulder. Omar, Aaron and Ace nod in agreement.

I scan the pages of ideas I put together while I was away from the island.

"Maybe we should do this at the hut," I suggest, suddenly feeling nervous. I spent the entire school term thinking of ideas for the gang, but now I am here in front of them, I'm afraid they won't take me seriously.

Omar looks out at the rain then back at me. "It's pouring down," he grumbles, pointing, as though I haven't seen the sheets of rain or heard it pelting down on the roof. "Let's do it here."

"You're a big boy, you can handle rain," Aaron says, patting his brother on the back.

I go over to the sliding door, pull the handle and fling it open. The rain sprays inside, soaking my face. I throw a blanket over my head and turn to the others. "We can shelter together under this blanket. It's not far."

Omar looks unconvinced, grimacing at the rain as though there might be a monster hiding outside.

Gaby and Ace both join me under the blanket.

"Leave him," Aaron says, pulling the blanket round him too. "He can stay here by myself, watching Elma cook or Dad work."

Omar immediately comes over. "Fine, but I go in the middle."

"Well, I'm holding the folder, so someone else needs to be at the end, and me in the middle," I argue.

Omar grabs the folder out of my hand. "I'm in the middle," he repeats, firmly placing himself between me and Aaron. It's not worth arguing over, so I let him have his way, pulling the end of the blanket over us.

"Ready?"

We run as fast as we can along the familiar stone path that leads to the hut. To the left of us, pellets of rain bounce off the pool. The cream cushions on the pool furniture are turning a dark grey.

We try, but it's impossible to fit under the blanket with five of us. Aaron runs ahead, sheltering his head with his hands, and Ace follows him. By the time the rest of us reach the hut, the door is open and they are already inside, shaking the rain off their clothes.

"Why couldn't we have done this inside the house?" Omar moans, trying not to get wet as we run inside.

But nothing he says can dim the smile on my face. Not the screeching from Gaby that rain just went down her neck, or Omar moaning that now his shoes are ruined. None of it could spoil how happy I feel to be back here. Back home, it has always only been me. I have no brothers and sisters. I struggle to make any real friends, because no one understands me, a book-reading girl who creates adventures in her head.

Now I have four other people to hang out with and play detectives, just as I had always dreamt of. It is the best feeling in the world.

I stand inside the doorway of the hut, trying to squeeze water out of the blanket, but it's not much use. So I lie it in the corner of the room on a plastic bag that has a game of Monopoly inside. I close the door, and as I lock it I feel my smile grow broader.

I'm so glad we came to the hut. Being here erases all doubts or fears I have about being back on the island and back with the group. The hut feels safe, like a warm welcoming hug.

I turn to face the rest of the group, who are all shaking themselves dry. For a minute I listen to their loud chatter, moving around them to the front of the room by Tia's familiar desk. I run my fingers along its wooden edge, something Tia would never have let me do before.

But she isn't here to stop me.

I lean against the desk and fold my hands in front of me. "Right," I say, opening my folder. "Shall we start?"

I hand out copies of my list to everyone. "These are just ideas," I say, squinting at Omar. "We can discuss them, keep the ones we like and get rid of the ones we don't."

Gaby glances at the list. "This is very organized, Fayson."

I beam and take a deep breath. "Idea number one—everyone gets a say, and we all make suggestions. I know when Tia was leader, she made the rules, but I think it works better if we all contribute." I glance up. "Unless you want me to be leader?" I ask hopefully.

"No," Omar says immediately. "No one wants that."

I look to the others, who all give half-hearted shrugs. "I like the idea that we all lead," Gaby says gently.

I bite my bottom lip, returning my gaze to the folder.

"Number two—I think we should have a rule about bullying. No making people feel like their ideas or their opinions don't matter. If you don't like what another member is doing, bring it to the group. We should deal with it together.

"Number three—everyone has a role. I think we can all bring a unique skill to the group.

Four—check in with each other, even when we go home. We have to be a gang that trusts each other. When we are close, we work better together."

I don't tell them that I got that straight out of my *How To Be a Villain* detective book.

"Five—if we want our detective agency to work, we need to canvass the island. Talk to people and let them know we're here in case they need us. We need to put the word out."

(Also stolen from one of my books.)

"I can do flyers," Ace suggests.

"Yes! He's really good at design," Gaby agrees.

I nod. "Okay, Ace will do all the design and admin for Di Island Crew. Gaby, maybe you can be the first contact for the club, the person people call if they need help?"

Gaby nods enthusiastically. "I do know everyone. And I don't mean to brag, but I'm pretty sure all the adults around here like me."

Omar snorts and Aaron digs his elbow into him, glaring at his brother so hard that Omar doesn't argue back.

"Aaron, maybe you can be the mediator for the group?" I suggest. "The one crew members go to if they have a problem."

Aaron raises his eyebrows, surprised, then blushes. "Yeah, I can do that," he says.

Omar frowns. "And what about me?"

"I thought you could be the hut keeper," I suggest.

Omar purses his lips, deep in thought. "Like a cleaner?"

I shake my head, remembering Mama and how upset she got when I suggested she come to the island to clean. "No, we'll all help with the chores, but you check on the hut and make sure no one breaks in."

"Oh, like a boss?" he says, a smile creeping on to his face.

"A hut keeper," Aaron says, cutting him

short. "Not a boss. We're all equals in the gang now, remember?"

"Like a supervisor," I say. He falls silent, thinking it over.

Gaby raises her hand. "Um, can we discuss the last suggestion on your list?"

I nod, looking down at the paper.

"You're kidding!" Omar says, reading it.

"It will ruin everything," Gaby cries.

"It will never work," Ace agrees, shaking his head.

I underlined the last point about twenty times, because even I wasn't sure they would go for it. But I had to do what was right.

"Yes, I know it's controversial…" I agree. "But I really think we should bring back Tia."

Chapter 3

The room fills with shouts of indignation and disbelief.

I listen patiently, because I knew this would happen. I knew this would be the reaction. But when I spoke to Mama about it, she said everyone deserves a second chance. That Tia seemed more lost than bad, and I should set the example she needs.

I want Mama to be proud of me. Something has changed between us since I first came to the island. She grew distant when I talked to her about Aunty Desiree buying me a new dress, or Omar's expensive new trainers. She would nod, makes a few sounds, then change the subject. But when I told her about Tia, Mama wanted to know more.

She asked me questions. And when I asked her what I should do with Tia, and whether she should be allowed back in our group, Mama replied: "Sounds like she needs more people like you around her." It was the first time I felt she was interested in Lighthouse Island. I want to keep it that way, and show her I can do the right thing.

"I think we should give Tia a second chance," I shout over their voices.

"Why?" Gaby cries. "She's not a nice person."

"I think, deep down, she can be nice," I argue.

Gaby shakes her head adamantly. "She's not. I'm telling you because I know her. I've known her much longer than you, Fayson. She's always been like this. Tia will never change."

The others nod their heads in agreement, except for Aaron. I look to him for help. "What do you think, Aaron? You're the mediator. Should we bring her back?"

Aaron glances up at me, then at Gaby who is glaring at him. Aaron sighs, shrugging his shoulders. "I dunno, I kind of agree with Fayson."

The others look at him in disbelief.

"She was horrible about Fayson, about all of us," Gaby reminds him.

Aaron nods his head slowly. "I know, I remember." He pauses, fidgeting with his hands. "But this is Tia's group really, she started it. None of this would have happened without her. Maybe she's changed?"

Gaby shakes her head furiously. "She never changes."

"Why don't we put it to a vote?" Ace suggests.

I look around the group and see how disheartened they are now. All the excitement from earlier has gone.

36

"Why don't we sleep on it, and come back tomorrow?" I suggest. "It's been a long day of travelling."

"Why don't you stop bossing us around," Omar grunts, getting to his feet. "You're like Tia 2.0."

I glare at the back of his head as he leaves, my heart stinging a little. Last time we were all here together, Tia was mean and selfish. She never thought about anyone but herself. It is why no one is talking to her right now. All I want is to do the right thing. To be the best detective. To be a great friend, and a daughter Mama is proud of.

To be compared to Tia is the worst thing Omar could have said to me.

The rain has stopped by the time we leave the hut. The mood is quiet, much different from when we first arrived, and I feel bad that it is because I brought up Tia. Clearly it was too soon for them to forgive her. Maybe it wasn't my place to ask them. Or maybe they are right to not trust her. Like Gaby said, I've only spent one school break with Tia. They have known her since they were eight years old.

As we reach the fork in the path, Gaby and Ace say their goodbyes. Gaby gives me a weak hug, which isn't like her.

"Are you okay?" I ask. She avoids my eyes, shrugging her shoulders.

"I don't understand why you want her back, when she was the meanest to you," she says, turning to catch up with Ace and not giving me time to answer.

I continue up the steps with Aaron beside me and Omar just ahead. As we reach the house I turn to Aaron. "Do you think I'm making a mistake wanting her back?"

"Yeah. You suck," Omar says, disappearing into the house.

I turn to Aaron. He offers me a weak shrug. "I don't know why you want her back, Fayson, she made our lives hell."

I'm confused. "But you said you agreed with me, in the hut."

"I'm the mediator, aren't I?" he says, raising his eyebrows. "I'm mediating. But for the record, I don't want her back either. The group is just better without her."

I watch in dismay as he enters the house through the living room doors.

All I want is to make Mama proud, to show her that I am still listening to her even when we are miles apart. I want to give Mama a reason to be happy that I am here, and then maybe she might want to come here herself next time. But this group is important to me too.

I want to make everyone happy. I'm just not sure I know how to do that.

*

We sit in silence eating sandwiches. Omar is throwing daggers at me from across the room, while Aaron stares outside, in between bites of chicken pattie. Uncle Edmond is eating in his office while he works, and Aunty Desiree has taken a basket of guineps, which she picked from the tree in the garden, over to the neighbours.

Elma opens the doors that lead out into the back garden, and a gentle breeze floats into the living room. I take a bite of sandwich, staring at the pool, but my mind is filled with thoughts of Tia and how upset the group are with me.

Omar picks up a slice of fried plantain from his plate, still glaring at me, and bites down on it.

"Are you going to keep staring at me like that?" I ask him.

He throws another chip in his mouth and purposely chews loudly, with a tilt of his head. "Are you going to keep talking about Tia coming back?"

I sigh, pushing my chair back and standing. "You're so immature," I say, taking my plate and leaving the table.

"You're immature!" Omar shouts after me, as I head out the door and on to the patio.

I walk over to the pool, lowering myself down and sitting on the edge. I take my shoes and socks off, allowing my bare feet to dangle in the cool water.

In my favourite *Hazley and Barnaby* detective book, Hazley didn't find it so hard to be in a detective agency. In fact Barnaby, her dog, was a very easy companion.

I sigh again, picking up my plate and taking a bite of my sandwich. Maybe I should be in a group with a dog, not humans.

I am staring out into the horizon, daydreaming of solving mysteries with a loyal dog, when I feel a sudden push from behind. I wobble precariously, trying to hold on to my plate, but before I can stop myself, I fall head first into the pool. The plate falls out of my hand and I sink under the water before fighting my way to the surface, coughing and spluttering.

Omar stands on the edge, throwing his head back in laughter. "Your face!" he squeals, pointing at me.

I glare at him as I paddle the water to stay afloat.

"I could have died!" I scream at him, but this only makes him laugh harder. He bends forward, holding his stomach.

Aaron approaches, a sandwich in his hand. He looks at me, then at his brother bent over laughing, before giving Omar a quick push and sending him flying into the pool beside me.

Omar reappears on the surface, his face fuming. Aaron chuckles, stuffing the last bit of food in his mouth. Which makes me chuckle too.

"What did you do that for?" Omar screams at his brother.

Aaron shrugs. "You deserved it."

Omar swims to the edge of the pool and pulls himself out. He glares at his grinning brother. "You're gonna regret that," he threatens, storming towards him like a bull.

Aaron turns on his heels, running away from the pool. He zips from left to right along the grass, trying to confuse his brother, who only becomes more determined by the second. I climb out of the pool, looking down at my clothes, which are dripping wet, and the half-eaten sandwich now floating in the pool.

"Fayson!" Aaron calls. "Help!" I don't need any more encouragement; I chase after Omar as we both try to corner him.

"What is going on here!" Aunty Desiree's voice cuts through our squeals of laughter. We stop abruptly, guilt written all over our faces. She stares at our wet clothes in horror, then at the pool with the upturned plate and floating sandwich.

"Get inside," she orders, pointing towards the house. "And don't get my floor wet!"

I enter my room through the glass sliding doors, and tiptoe across the tiled floor towards the bathroom to get a towel.

Inside the dark oak bathroom, I change into a pair of shorts and T-shirt, throwing my wet clothes into the bath, just as I would do at home. It's where Mama always tells me to wash my clothes.

With a towel wrapped around my hair, I re-enter the bedroom, worried that Aunty Desiree might phone Mama and tell her I'm not behaving. I have only been here for a couple of hours and already I could be sent home.

As I pass the bedroom door, an object catches my eye. A piece of paper has been pushed under my door from the hallway. I walk over and bend down, staring at the folded piece of paper before picking it up. Walking over to the bed, I sit down on the edge, unfolding the paper.

My eyes scan the words and my heart flutters. It's only a few lines, typed, but it is enough to make me lose my breath.

I KNOW YOUR SECRET.
I KNOW THE TRUTH ABOUT LIZZY.

I stare at the paper in disbelief. Who could know about what happened with Lizzy? I told no one. The only person who knew besides me was Mama, and she would never betray me. So, who else could it be? Who found out my secret, and how?

I read it over and over again, with my hand over my mouth. The only people who knew about Lizzy were Mama… and Gaby. Mama would never write this, but Gaby?

My heart sinks to the pit of my stomach. I've told her all my secrets, details no one else knows about me…

But Gaby is my best friend. She swore to never tell another soul, and I believe her. I shake the thought away, Gaby would never do this, we've become so close we're like sisters. We swore to always have each other's back. She would be devastated if she knew I had even considered her doing this! It has to be someone else.

Forcing myself to stand, I tiptoe over to the door and yank it open to see if whoever wrote the note is still outside. As I peer out, I see Aaron looking out from his bedroom too.

Aaron? Could it be him? But how would he know about Lizzy? I didn't trust him or Omar with any of my secrets.

He looks at me strangely.

"You okay?" he asks in weird flat tone.

I nod slowly, my heart still pounding, "Yeah, I'm fine," I say, trying to spot a clue in his face. Maybe Mama told Uncle Edmond, and Uncle Edmond told Aunty Desiree and Aaron overheard them.

"Are you… fine?" I ask suspiciously. He nods slowly.

There's the sound of a door opening and Omar steps out. He stops suddenly when he sees us. We both turn to him, and I squint at him suspiciously. He squints back at me. Then he slides out of his room with his back against the wall.

"What are you two doing?" he asks, dragging the words out slowly.

"What are *you* doing?" I shoot back, wondering how it could be Omar, when he would be the last person I would trust with a secret. But even if Omar found out from someone else, he wouldn't keep it a secret and send me notes. Omar is the type of person who blurts out whatever you tell him to whoever is listening. He couldn't keep a secret if he tried.

"I asked first," he says, shooting glares from me to Aaron.

"I heard Fayson's door," Aaron says, "so I came to see what she was doing."

I scowl at him. "Can't I open my door? Are you the house police?" I step out of the room, folding my arms across my chest. "And anyway, you were already out of your room when I opened mine," I snap.

Elma comes round the corner with a pile of towels in her arms. She stops when she sees us, her eyebrows wrinkling.

"Is everyone okay?"

I force a smile, even though I am panicking inside. "Yes, Elma, we're fine."

"We were just talking," Aaron adds.

"About food," Omar says.

We all look at him.

"Are you still hungry?" Elma asks. "I can make you another snack."

We all shake our heads in unison. "No thank you, Elma," I tell her. "We're not hungry."

She narrows her eyes. "Okay…" she says, as she passes us to get to the linen cupboard next to Omar's room. I watch as she opens the door and places the towels in, disappearing for a second before reappearing to catch me staring.

I quickly rush into my room and close the door. Seconds later I hear two other doors close at the same time.

I lean against the door, my mind racing. Elma? Could it be Elma? I shake the thought away immediately. No, not Elma, she is way too kind.

So that leaves Aaron and Omar. Both have played horrible tricks on me in the past, but since I came to the island, Aaron hasn't upset me. In fact, he's been kind to me. I was beginning to see him as a friend.

I sit on the floor with my legs crossed, staring at the letter, my elbows on my knees.

It could be Omar, but he is more into harmless tricks than being mean.

If it is Omar, how would he know my secret? Omar is annoying, but he isn't the FBI. They brought me to the island for that very reason, to help them solve the mystery at the lighthouse. He couldn't find out my secret by himself.

There is a short knock on my door and it opens before I can answer. Aunty Desiree peers in.

"Your mother is on the phone," she says.

My heart sinks. As if things couldn't get any worse. I get to my feet and she beckons me out. I follow her into the hall.

"She called Edmond's office phone," Aunty Desiree says, her brows wrinkling.

I follow her down the hall, puzzled. Why didn't Mama call my phone? I feel a sudden dread. Aunty Desiree must have sent Mama a message. Mama rarely answers her phone first time, she's always too busy working.

Aunty Desiree turns to me. "And when you're done, you and the boys need to clean that pool," she says before going outside.

I walk through the living room and to the other side of the house. When I get to Uncle Edmond's office, I turn the handle on the large office door and enter. He looks up and I try to read his expression, but Uncle Edmond is really hard to read.

"Sit down, Fayson," Uncle Edmond says.

I do as I'm told and sit on the chair facing his large oak desk.

He stares at me for some seconds. "Your mother called to see if you got here safely," he says, leaning back in his chair. "She must think we live a foreign," he says in Patwah, chuckling.

I raise my eyebrows, shocked to hear him speak like that when he is always correcting my English.

A sigh comes from down the phone and I hear Mama kissing her teeth. She's on speakerphone. *"You don't have to live a foreign for something to happen,"* she says. *"It can happen on your back door. I want to know if my only child got there safe, that's all."*

Uncle Edmond nods to me. "Well, let her tell to you for herself," he says.

I sit forward in the chair, a little confused as to why Mama has called me on Uncle Edmond's phone.

"Mama, I'm okay," I say loudly to the speaker.

"Good," she says.

There is a long pause.

"Well, I'll let you go then," she says. "You can call me anytime, Fayson. You know that, don't you?"

I nod. "Yes, Mama."

"Be good."

"Yes, Mama."

She clears her throat. "Look after her, Edmond," she says, and then the line goes dead.

I raise my eyes to look at Uncle Edmond. He sits forward, resting his elbows on the desk.

"Well, that was nice," he says, then turns to his computer and begins tapping away.

Why did Mama phone Uncle Edmond and not me? I had thought it was because I was in trouble, but I'm not.

I push the chair back and leave the room, pausing outside.

Maybe Mama didn't want to speak to me. Maybe she wanted to speak to Uncle Edmond. If she wanted to speak to Uncle Edmond, she must not hate him any more. And if she doesn't hate him any more, Mama might come to the island.

I try not to get too excited, taking a deep breath to calm myself down, but maybe, just maybe, I might get Mama to Lighthouse Island after all!

Chapter 4

As I walk back through the house from my
uncle's office, no one is around except for Elma
in the kitchen. She spots me as I walk by.

"Ms Fayson!" she calls brightly. "I'm making
some coconut drops, come try one."

I enter the kitchen, still thinking about
Mama's phonecall and why she called Uncle
Edmond and not me. I thought I was in
trouble!

Elma hands me a small coconut drop from
a plate on the kitchen island. She watches as

I take a bite into the tough but sweet dessert that has pieces of hard coconut sticking out of it.

"You like it?" she asks. I nod, trying hard not to get it stuck in my teeth.

"I love it," I tell her. "Mama makes them sometimes too."

Elma smiles widely, wiping down the kitchen sides. "I think your Mama and I would get along," she says.

I nod, catching a glimpse of an open door on the other side of the kitchen. The door that leads to Elma's apartment. Music plays softly from a radio inside. I think how Elma and I could be neighbours; her apartment here is the same size as our apartment back home.

"Whose phone is that?" Elma asks, as she hears ringing. I listen. It sounds like it's coming from down the hall. I hurry out of the kitchen. That's my phone, I would recognize the ringtone anywhere.

"Thank you, Elma!" I shout, as I hurry towards my room.

I reach for the phone on my bed and check the number. I'm surprised to see it's Ace. He never calls me.

"Hello Ace," I say, when he picks up.

"I've done them," he says.

I wait for more information but get none. "Done what?" I ask patiently, almost glad for the distraction.

"The flyers!" he says, as if I should have known. "I've done them. We can deliver them now."

"Now?" I look out the window at the dark skies. The storm has passed. It's after six in the evening and still light despite the clouds from the storm. We have a few more hours before it gets dark, but it could rain again any minute.

"Yes, I'm outside," he says.

I stand up, walking over to the glass doors. Sure enough, there he is, waiting in the side porch. He's wearing a bright yellow hoodie covering his usually curly hair, and holding a wad of papers in his hand. He waves them at me.

I open the door and step out, staring at him. "Ace, you didn't have to do them now."

He shrugs. "I was bored, and this was easy." He hands me a bunch of flyers. "It only took ten minutes."

I smile, reading the top flyer.

Something strange you can't explain?
Someone lost, who needs to be found?
Di Island Crew will investigate!
Call us now!!
No job too small, no case too hard.

The letters are in large stencil fonts, and bright green, yellow and black colours. He has used his computer to illustrate five people investigating, like you might see in a detective movie. One person has a phone to their ear, the other a magnifying glass to their eye. One holds a pen and notebook, another is sat behind a computer, and the last one is knocking on a door. The rest of the paper shows the image of a lighthouse with a flashing light, footprints and a cat running.

I beam at him. "Ace, this is amazing!"

He shrugs, avoiding my eyes. "It's nothing special."

I shake my head, staring at the flyer in awe. "It's more than special. This is going to get us the best cases, I can feel it."

A small smile pulls at his lips and he straightens his posture. "So... shall we go deliver them?" he suggests.

I could really do with a distraction from the Lizzy note and all the friction at the house.

"Definitely."

*

Back inside, I throw on the old worn-down trainers Mama bought me last Christmas and a dark grey jacket, because the air is a little cool after the rain. I join Ace and we walk round the outside of the house and down the driveway to the road.

I realize, as we walk in silence, that Ace and I have never spent any time alone. It was always as part of the group. He's closer to the boys and isn't very talkative. He walks beside me with his head down, his eyes scanning the ground in front of him. As we come to the end of the driveway he turns left on to the road.

"We should start on this side and work our way round the island," he says, waving his hand in a circular motion.

I nod. "That sounds like a good idea."

We continue up the road until we reach the first house on the left.

"Why don't we play a game?" I suggest as we approach the first house, a sprawling one-storey home set back just off the road.

"Okay," he says slowly, dragging out the word. We walk up the short path.

"It's a get-to-know-you game that we play at school," I explain.

Ace groans as we approach the bright-yellow front door, then knocks. "I hate those stupid games," he says, making a face.

Before I can ask him his first question, the front door opens and a woman with short black hair opens the door. She steps forward and looks from me to Ace, smiling.

"Ace," she says in a sing-song voice, "how have you been?"

"Good," Ace mumbles, handing her the flyer.

As the woman reads it, her eyebrows raise. "You're a detective now? That's very exciting." She looks up at me and gives me a slight nod. "You're Fayson."

I nod back, wondering how she knows.

"I remember you from last summer," she says, giving me a wink. "You interrupted our lunch to tell on Tia and her very naughty behaviour." She folds the flyer into two. "Well, I don't have a case for you yet, but I'll be sure to let you know when I do."

We leave the house and return to the road.

"So, first question," I say, picking the game back up. "Do you have any brothers or sisters?"

"I have a little brother who is eight months old."

My head jerks back. "You have a brother?"

Ace shrugs it away. "Yeah, he's just *there* though. Doesn't really do much except eat, sleep and make random sounds." He proceeds to make gurgling sounds like his throat is full of water, which makes me smile as we walk on.

"Babies are a bit pointless until they can talk," he adds. "I love him though."

We follow the curve of the road to the left, then it becomes straight and I can see the back of Uncle Edmond's garden. His familiar banana tree sways in the gentle breeze.

"This is Mr Devan and his wife's place." Ace points to the right, at a red roof peeking out from bushes and overgrown trees.

We cross the road and approach. It looks so different from the other houses, which are well kept, with mowed grass and perfect gardens. We fight our way through the bushes and overgrown trees.

"They are both scientists. They're different from most people here; they don't like being conventional. But they're really nice, and Mr Devan likes to DJ whenever we have parties."

The front door is overgrown with ferns. Ace bangs his knuckles against the door.

"His wife, Bernadette, thinks she's some world-class dancer too." He barely finishes before the door opens and a tall man stands in the doorway, his head grazing the top of the door.

"Ace!" the man cries, grabbing Ace into a tight hug. He lets Ace go and grabs me just as tightly. "I can't remember your name," he says in a booming voice. "But I remember that face!" He grins, mischievously wagging his finger at me. "Come in, come in. Bernie just made some tea."

"We're not staying," Ace tries to tell him, but Mr Devan pushes us both inside and closes the door.

"Bernadette, we have visitors!" he shouts.

A woman appears from around the corner, her head partly covered by a head tie, wearing a matching blouse and a pleated skirt.

"Oh, you're just in time," she declares. "I've made some sweet tea."

"That's what I said," Mr Devan replies, and they both beam at us.

"We're not staying," Ace repeats, louder this time. He shoves a flyer into Mr Devan's hands.

Mr Devan takes it just as Mrs Devan joins him and they both read it.

"A detective agency!" Mr Devan says, his eyes wide. He taps the paper. "I always wanted to be a detective."

Mrs Devan shakes her head, walking away. "No, you didn't."

"Yes I did!" Mr Devan shouts, following her, and they both continue to argue, disappearing down the hall.

Ace and I leave quickly, before they come back, and as soon as we are far enough away, we dissolve into hysterical laughter.

"Next question… What's your favourite colour?" I ask, continuing the game.

"Blue."

"Favourite country?"

"This country!" he says.

"What do your parents do for a living?"

Ace falls silent, and I have to peer at him to see if he even heard me. I ask again but he seems distracted.

"We're here," he says, nodding to the house

on the right. "This is Mrs Hammond's. She's pretty weird."

I sneak a glance at him as we open the iron gates and walk up the gravel path.

"So, what do your parents do?" I ask again. We reach the front door and he knocks, avoiding my eyes.

"Not everything is about money, Fayson," he says quietly.

I frown. "I know that."

He turns away from me, looking out over Mrs Hammond's brick wall, his arms folded across his chest. When no one answers, Ace shoves a flyer under the door and walks off. I run after him, puzzled.

We return to the road and the mood between us feels different. He walks a little ahead of me in silence, the bunch of flyers crushed slightly in his right fist. The road veers downwards towards the sea, and not far in the distance I can see Tia's house looming above the trees.

Finally Ace slows down enough for me to catch him up. As we turn the corner, there is a figure leaning against the wall of Tia's house.

"Oh no," Ace whispers under his breath, as we both recognize who it is: Tia. She stands at the bottom of the road, about twenty feet from us. "Look," he says, not taking his eyes off her. "Let's treat this vacation like it's our last. Let's do everything we want to and make the most of this detective club."

I shoot him a glance. "Why, aren't you coming back?"

He shakes his head, passing the flyers from one hand to the other, his eyes not leaving Tia. "You just never know, you know, if any of us will return," he says quietly.

I think about Mama wanting me to come here the first time, but the second time not being so happy about it. I think about Uncle Edmond and Aunty Desiree, and how it always feels like they could send me home any minute.

I feel Ace's arm touch mine as we get closer to Tia, and I don't move away because it feels warm and comforting. As though he's sharing something with me that he's never shared with anyone.

"What are you two doing?" Tia shouts, squinting at us. We slow down as we approach her. Before either of us can answer, she reaches towards Ace and yanks one of the flyers out of his hand. She reads it.

"So you're doing the club without me," she says, her eyes fixed on the paper. Ace stares at his feet.

"We all know you started it, Tia," I tell her, clenching my jaw, "and you're welcome to come back if you promise to be nice."

She sucks in her cheeks. "Who says I want to be in your stupid gang? Maybe I have a better gang that's going to blow your gang out of the water."

Ace makes a face. "With who?"

It's no secret we are the only kids our age around here.

Tia turns on her heels. "None of your business." She disappears through the side gate and into the trees that surround her house.

"You shouldn't have said that," Ace says as we walk away.

"Said what?" I ask, still thinking about Tia forming a new gang. Maybe she's brought new people on to the island, or maybe she's bluffing. It's hard to know with Tia. She has the power to create an entirely new group if she wanted to, but she's also known for telling lies.

"You shouldn't have told Tia she could come back," Ace replies. "It's not only your decision to make."

"I knew she wouldn't want to," I retort. I bite my lip, stealing a glance at him, but he doesn't answer.

We deliver our last flyer to Thompson the caretaker. If we're going to get any cases on this island, Thompson will most likely be the one to find them for us.

When we approach his tiny wooden house, all the memories from last summer come flooding back. The footprints, the lighthouse and sneaking into Thompson's house to steal his boots.

"I missed out on the mission to Thompson's house," Ace says, laughing as I remind him. "I was busy keeping guard, remember?" I do remember, and I feel a little guilty that he wasn't part of it.

Thompson doesn't answer his door, which isn't surprising as he is always patrolling the island. Ace grabs a stone from his front yard and places the last flyer on his rickety porch with the stone on top to stop it flying away.

On the way back home, I try to ask Ace more questions to get to know him, but he seems reluctant, so eventually I give up. We reach my cousins' house and stop at the entrance of the driveway. Ace stares at his feet again.

"This was fun," I tell him, trying to lighten the mood. He nods, kicking a stone on the ground. "And nothing's going to change," I tell him. "We'll all be back next school holidays, you'll see."

He nods again, then turns on his heel, heading home.

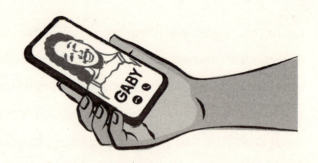

Chapter 5

I wake the next morning to my phone ringing.
I reach over to the bedside table and feel
around until my hands wrap around it. I peer at
the screen through blurry eyes.

It's Gaby.

I lift the phone to my ear, my face half buried
by the pillow.

"Hello?"

"Hey, Fayson." She sounds breathless.

"You okay?" I ask sleepily, remembering how
last time I saw her she was unhappy with me
for wanting to bring Tia back.

There is a pause. "Yes, I'm great. You?" she replies, in her usual cheery voice.

I glance at the note about Lizzy, which is on the floor. Reaching down with my other hand I pick it up and shove it into the top drawer. "Yeah. Some weird things going on, but..." I trail off, not knowing whether to tell Gaby about the note.

"Like what?"

Her voice comes through the phone crisp and loud, as though she has the phone closer to her mouth than before.

"Fayson, what happened?"

I roll on to my back, wiping the sleep from my eyes. I haven't been able to stop thinking about the note and who could have written it. Last night, as I walked round the island with Ace, I wondered if it was him. When we bumped into Tia, I thought it was probably her. Even last night I looked at Aaron and Omar suspiciously.

Should I tell Gaby about the note? What if she wrote it?

I shake the thought out of my head. She wouldn't. Gaby is my best friend. The one person in our group who I trust the most.

I clear my throat. "Just home stuff," I tell her, which isn't a lie. It is about home. Lizzy is from home.

"Your mum?" she asks, sounding worried.

I shake my head, as though she can see me. "No, other stuff. Stuff you wouldn't understand."

Neither of us speak for a moment. I pull myself up to sitting, leaning against the back wall and staring at the wooden beams across the ceiling. I want to tell Gaby about the letter so much. But if I tell her about the letter, I will have to tell her about my secret.

"So why did you call?" I ask, breaking the silence.

"Oh yeah. Ace told me you dropped

the flyers off, but you didn't speak to Mrs Hammond. So I went over there myself."

I look at the time on my phone. "Why? It's so early."

"I know, I know," she says, her voice rising with excitement. "I couldn't help it! No one has ever given me such an important role before."

"Okay, but—"

"Don't be mad, but I got us our first client!"

Wow, that was quick!

I sit up straight. I'm a little disappointed she went off by herself and didn't tell the rest of us, but Omar's words about being a Tia 2.0 are still ringing in my ears, so I try my best to sound pleased. "You did? Who?"

Besides, she got us a client, and that's what we all want.

"Mrs Hammond," Gaby replies, talking so quickly I can barely keep up with her. "She keeps to herself usually and rarely comes to any of our parties. She takes two walks at the same time every day, seven in the morning and seven in the evening. But if you catch her at the right moment, she will stop and talk to you."

"And you caught her on her walk?" I asked.

Gaby hesitates. "No, but her door was unlocked so I let myself in."

"Gaby!" I cry in horror. "You can't walk into people's houses. That's how people disappear in my detective books."

"I know, I know," she admits. "She wasn't very happy at first, but when I told her we solve mysteries no matter how big or small, she said she may have a mystery at her house for us to solve."

I lean into the phone. "Really?" I whisper breathlessly.

"Yes!" she screeches down the phone, and I wish I could reach in and hug her. "We have a case and I really think we should go over there soon, before she changes her mind."

I agree, swinging my legs out of bed. "You tell Ace and I'll tell the twins. Then we'll meet at Mrs Hammond's house in an hour."

The five of us stand in front of Mrs Hammond's house. It is different to the other houses I've seen on the island. They are all modern white stone, with swimming pools and large backyards. Mrs Hammond's house is old, like the kind of old where ghosts live.

I pay more attention to the house than I did last night. There are grey slabs on the roof that are stained and cracking, and the front of the bright yellow house sticks out, with a small porch. Wooden shutters cover two windows either side of the entrance, with two porches, one at the front and another to the side of the house. Wide, flat steps lead down from the side porch to a gate, with a small garden and flowers of every colour around the edges.

"So, she's not mean, she just doesn't like people?" I confirm for the second time, as we stand outside the gate.

"She can be a little mean," Omar grumbles.

"I think she just likes to be by herself," Aaron comments, as we survey the house.

"She's really nice when you get to know her," Gaby adds. "You just have to know how to talk to her. I know how to talk to her."

"Bighead," Omar coughs.

Gaby glares at him for a second, but then her smile returns. "She says she's had a strange sound coming from her wardrobe way before any of us moved to the island. She thought the sound would stop, but it hasn't."

"Why didn't she tell anyone?" I ask.

"She doesn't talk to anyone, duh." Omar says.

"Mrs Hammond says sometimes she doesn't even hear the sounds now, as she's so used to it," Gaby explains.

I stare at the looming house. The shutters are closed. I take a deep breath. "Alright, let's go."

Gaby leads us through the gate, and up the grey stone steps. We all crowd on to the porch behind her. She knocks firmly three times and stands back.

We wait, but there is no answer. Gaby knocks again.

"Didn't you say she doesn't answer the door?" I ask.

She half turns to look at me, with a knowing smile. "Yes, but I think it's polite always to knock before walking in."

Gaby is about to turn the handle when the door opens. She jumps back.

"Mrs Hammond!" she gasps.

A small woman with big curly white hair and almond-coloured eyes looks out at us.

"Yes?"

She is wearing a flowery dress, buttoned up to her neck, and a necklace with a large green stone that sits on her chest. There are lots of lines on her face that tell me she's old, but her face is soft and round, which makes her look like a young person in old-people make-up.

I nudge Gaby and she steps forward.

"Mrs Hammond, it's me Gaby."

Mrs Hammond gives a short nod of her head, "Yes, I know who you are," she says. "Do you think I forgot you already?"

"We're Di Island Crew," I tell her proudly. I have been waiting so long to say that. It feels official now, like we are the real deal.

She looks at us. "I know all of you." Her eyes stop on me and her eyebrows wrinkle. "But I don't know you."

I open my mouth to introduce myself, but Gaby gets there first. "Mrs Hammond, this is Fayson. She's very good at solving mysteries."

Mrs Hammond offers me her hand to shake. "Nice to meet you, Fayson-who-is-good-at-solving-mysteries."

I spot a twinkle in her eye and chuckle. "Nice to meet you, Mrs Hammond."

She turns, walking through the living room and down the hall. "Come in, come in."

The five of us follow hesitantly, looking around. We weave through a room full of chairs of different shapes and sizes. There are three different armchairs, all yellow, a blue sofa with white flowers, with a footstool in front of it, and four wooden chairs that look like part of a table set, but there's no table.

"Why does she need so many chairs?" Aaron whispers, as if reading my mind.

I shrug. "Maybe she collects them?"

"No one collects chairs," Omar retorts, running his hand over a grey velvet chair with a blue flower pattern.

"My grandma collects flowers," Ace says. "She dries them so that they'll last for ever. She has them all over her house. It looks like the botanical gardens in there!"

"It's not the same though, is it," Omar argues. "Flowers look good. You can put them anywhere. But this," he points around the room, "is bordering on weird."

"Just because you don't understand it doesn't mean it's weird," I snap. I'm getting sick of his comments. He hasn't stopped moaning and offering snide remarks since they left their home in the city and came to pick me up for this trip.

"*You're* weird," he retorts.

I roll my eyes, and I'm about to tell him to try harder when a gentle voice interrupts us.

"So, I suppose you want to see the wardrobe?" It's Mrs Hammond, who is standing in the far doorway at the end of the hall.

Gaby follows Mrs Hammond down the hall before we can answer.

"Well, are the rest of you coming?" Mrs Hammond calls. We rush to catch up with her at the end of the corridor.

Behind her is a window that looks out into the backyard. Unlike the front of the house, the space is filled with trees, and you can barely see the ground.

"My husband and I moved here when I retired from teaching," she says. "We wanted to get away from the city, away from all the noise." She beams as she remembers. "The island was owned by a foreign gentleman back then. He wasn't particularly interested in it. It had been passed down to him from his father. He didn't care who lived here, as long as it was looked after. My husband and I agreed to be the caretakers of

Lighthouse Island, way before Thompson was given the job.

"There was no one here when we first came, before the Brookes bought the island and brought all the city folks with them. They let us stay, so we were grateful for that." She lays her hand on the door. "My husband had all sorts of interests, but he particularly liked to fix any old junk he could find. This house has a unique room that allowed him to tinker away without disturbing me."

Mrs Hammond reaches a hand into her skirt pocket and pulls out a set of keys. She runs her fingers through the set and stops at a long brass key with a hollow head. It's much bigger than the other keys.

She slips the key into the door and turns it. The door creaks open.

I hold my breath as she switches on a faint light on the inside wall and descends a dark wooden staircase. I grip the bannister tightly, imagining what could be down there. A ghost?

A monster? Maybe her husband turned into a monster and she had to lock him away so he wouldn't hurt anyone.

I glance at the others, wide-eyed, but they don't seem to be as excited as I am.

Omar takes one step back, and Ace shakes his head adamantly, refusing to follow her. Gaby's smile wavers as she leans over my shoulder, trying to peer down the stairs.

I look to Aaron, the only other sensible one here. He stares at the open door, his mouth twisted.

"Well, are you coming?" Mrs Hammond calls up.

"Yes, Mrs Hammond, we're coming," I answer, trying to hide the excitement in my voice.

I lead the way down the wooden stairs, hoping it will reassure the rest of the group if I go first.

The stairs creak with every step, like in a creepy horror movie. The walls are so close either side that my shoulders almost touch both walls. When I reach the bottom, I am faced with a single lightbulb hanging from the ceiling. The walls are made of stone, painted white. The room feels cold.

The others follow hesitantly.

"This used to be the kitchen, back in the old days," Mrs Hammond tells us, looking around. "It's where the slaves were put to work. Back then, they had no light and no heat, except from the wood-burning fire."

There is a bitterness to her voice, but this quickly changes as she continues the story.

"My husband worked for hours down here, fixing everything you can think of."

We look around the cold, dark cellar. There are wooden shelves placed around the room, and every space is filled with odd bits and pieces. Old kettles, clocks, bicycle parts and some objects I don't even recognize.

"The one he really struggled with, though, was this one."

She leads us to the back of the room where a dark brown wardrobe leans against the stone wall.

"There seemed to be a few minor issues with it. Just a few scratches, a hanging door, nothing that couldn't be easily fixed." She stands some distance from the wardrobe as she speaks. "But then he began hearing sounds coming from inside. It was so strange."

I move slowly towards the wardrobe to get a better look. Gaby grabs my shoulder, shaking her head and blinking rapidly.

I tilt my head, peering at the old wardrobe looming over us. It looks like any other cupboard you might see in your grandparents' house. Those typical old wooden wardrobes. Every grandmother in the country has one.

But I can feel something that makes the hairs on my arm stand on end.

Mrs Hammond lowers her voice. "Listen," she whispers.

We tilt our ears towards the wardrobe and listen. We stand in complete silence for what seems like for ever. It's the most quiet I have ever seen the group.

Finally Mrs Hammond breaks the silence with a grunt. "It must not want to perform for you today," she says, shaking her head. "You might have to return another time."

The others start to leave.

I beg whatever is inside to show itself— *Come on!*—but the room is silent. My shoulders slump, and reluctantly I turn away.

A noise explodes into the room, from the wardrobe. Everyone stops in their tracks. My whole body stiffens. It's a sound I was not expecting. It's a sound that sends chills down my spine.

It is the sound of someone knocking.

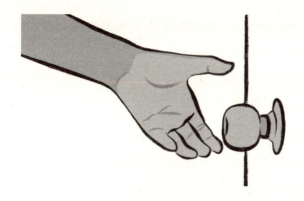

Chapter 6

"Oh there it is," Mrs Hammond cries, sounding delighted by the ghostly knocking. "Our friend must be playing games with you. It can be quite the comedian!"

The knocking continues, like a hammer against a wall.

My heart rings in my ears, as I force myself to turn back and face the wardrobe. My breath is loud, and my hands ball into fists. I edge closer.

"Fayson…" Gaby's trembling voice calls me back, but I barely hear her. It's as if a magnetic field is pulling me. No matter how frightened I am, I must see where the sound is coming from.

The noise continues as I get closer. *Thud, thud, thud*, in a slow rhythm, like a tired old man with his cane across the floor.

I lift my right hand slowly, resting it on the door of the wardrobe. I run my hand along the dark wood until it curls round the handle. I take a deep breath and yank the door open.

The noise stops.

My chest rises and falls rapidly, and it takes some time for it to slow.

I peer inside the wardrobe. It is empty apart from an old grey coat on a single hanger, and a wooden chest placed against the back of the wardrobe. I turn to the others, who are waiting anxiously on the other side of the room.

"There's no one here," I tell them.

The others rush over and peer inside. Aaron presses his hand against the inside of the wardrobe.

Omar actually climbs inside, feeling around with his hands. He slides back out seconds later, dusting his hands off. "Nope, just some old chest," he says.

I turn to Mrs Hammond, who is watching us, bemused, at the bottom of the stairs.

"We will need to go away and discuss our findings," I tell her, giving her a short nod.

She starts back up the steps. "Well, I'm happy to give you kids a task to do in your school holidays."

We follow her back up the stairs. She locks the door behind her with the old key, placing it in her pocket, then leads us out.

"We will need to come back, Mrs Hammond," Gaby says to her.

Mrs Hammond nods, already closing the front door. "Yes, yes, whatever you need. Just not on a Wednesday. That is the time I spend with Alfred, my husband." She shuts the door.

We walk away in silence, our minds spinning.

"Isn't her husband... dead?" Ace whispers.

My eyes widen. "You tell me, you're the ones who know her!"

The others confer in hushed voices, as though Mrs Hammond can hear them. They all start nodding at the same time.

"Yeah, he's definitely dead." Aaron announces.

We continue along the road in silence, heading back to the hut. Omar jumps suddenly, screaming that something touched his neck, and starts to run. We race after him, too afraid to look back.

It's only when we are far away from Mrs Hammond's house that we slow down.

"Stop... I... can't... breathe..." Omar pants, bending over and grabbing his knees. We all slow down to catch our breath. Then, without mentioning a word about Mrs Hammond's dead husband, we walk silently back to the hut.

When we reach the hut, Omar orders us to wait before entering, while he walks round the outside. We watch blankly until he reappears, on the other side.

"What are you doing?" Aaron asks his brother irritably.

Omar gives him a cutting look. "Don't you remember what my job is? To keep the hut safe. So, I'm checking for safety," he says. "That is my job, isn't it?"

He looks to me and I bite my lip, forcing a smile down and giving him a short nod.

"Right," he says. "Stand back." We take a small step back while Omar unlocks the door of the hut and peers in. He enters, closing the door behind him.

Aaron groans, shaking his head. "This is ridiculous. See what you've done, Fayson? He's going to be a nightmare now!"

Minutes later, Omar pops his head round the door with a wide grin. "All good," he reports. "Coast is clear. You can all enter now."

One by one he allows us in. Aaron swipes at his brother's head as he passes, but Omar manages to duck out of the way. When everyone is inside, he closes the door behind us, but not before giving outside a quick check again.

We all sit on the floor, and I look at them with wide eyes, clasping my hands together to steady my fidgeting hands. "So, what do we think about Mrs Hammond's case? Shall we take it?"

The room erupts into excited chatter.

"I dunno," Omar says, shaking his head once the chatter has settled down. "It all seems a bit freaky to me."

"But isn't that what we want?" Gaby cries. "And we might never get a case like this again."

Gaby is right. What are the chances that we will get two big mysteries to solve, on such a tiny island?

"If we don't take this one, we might only get cases for missing goats, or finding rats in kitchens," I say.

Omar shudders. "Ugh, I hate rats."

Gaby waves her hands in front of us. "Guys, can we focus? Mrs Hammond is so nice. I really want to help her." The boys shoot her a look, but Gaby won't be swayed. "She was nice enough to let us into her house."

"The house with her dead husband," Omar adds.

"Did anyone know she spoke to her dead husband?" I ask, puzzled. After all, they have been here much longer than me.

"We've never talked to her except to say hello," Aaron explains. "Our parents invite her over all the time, but she always says no. Papa says she likes her own company."

"Now we know why she doesn't talk to anyone," Omar retorts.

I shake my head. "I don't think we should worry. She's just lonely, that's all."

"I agree," Ace says, joining the discussion for the first time. "She's an old lady who wants someone to talk to."

"I think she just liked me," Gaby says, grinning widely. "She didn't trust me when I first went over this morning, but now she sees that I'm nice, she trusts me. People say all sorts when they trust you."

She's right, and I think about the secrets I myself have told her. Secrets only Gaby and Mama know, about Lizzy, and for a moment I wonder again if it might be Gaby who wrote the note. I shake it away instantly. Of all the people here on this island, Gaby is the one I trust the most.

"Love yourself much?" Omar scoffs, shaking his head.

Gaby sticks her chin out, defiant. "Yes, I do, and you should too!"

Omar closes his eyes and breathes in sharply, loud snoring sounds escaping his mouth.

"So, shall we vote?" I ask, looking at each of them. I raise my hand in the air. "I vote yes. Whatever is going on in that house is scary, but that's what we do. We've done scary before. I really think we can do this."

Gaby raises her hand too. "I agree. I can't imagine what it must have been like to live with that sound. I really want to help Mrs Hammond."

Aaron raises his hand too, and so does Ace.

Everyone turns to Omar.

He peers at us from under his eyelids, then groans, raising his hand slowly. "Okay, fine," he grunts. "But if I see her dead husband, I'm gone."

I beam round the room, my heart skipping wildly. "So, this is our second case," I say breathlessly.

I grin widely. If only they knew how much of a dream this was for me. I have been preparing for a mystery like this my whole life.

"Question," Ace says, raising his hand. "Does anyone else think her husband is in that wardrobe? And that's why she talks to him, because he's stuck there?"

Gaby's hand flies to her mouth, and a cold shiver runs through me.

Chapter 7

"We have one more decision to make," I say to the group, trying to ignore the thought Ace has put in my head about Mrs Hammond and her husband. I must try to stay on track.

I take a breath, knowing what I'm going to say next will not go down well.

"The next agenda item to talk about is whether we want Tia to rejoin the group."

Groans echo around the hut.

I sigh. "Okay. Well, I'll tell you why I think she should come back. For one, she started this group. We're only here because of her."

"She didn't start it," Gaby interrupts me. Then she smiles apologetically. "We kind of all started it, together."

"She just made herself the leader," Aaron agrees.

I sigh, feeling frustrated. They aren't going to make this easy for me. But I promised Mama I would give Tia a second chance.

"Okay…" I say, changing tactics. "Don't you think Tia has been punished enough? She was kicked out of the group, humiliated in front of everyone, and had the one person she disliked the most stay."

I look at each of them in turn. "How much does she need to suffer before we let her back? How would you feel if it was you?"

Gaby picks up a stray blade of grass that someone brought in with their shoe. She focuses hard on it, her eyebrows pushed together and her lips jutting out.

"I'm surprised it's you who wants her back, Fayson. Tia was worse to you than any of us. She was really mean to you, don't you remember?"

Gaby pulls her eyes away from the blade of grass and fixes them on me intently.

I stare back at her, unsure as to what she is trying to do. Is she trying to embarrass me? Remind me that I am not the same as them?

"They were only words," I tell her, my mouth tightening. "I'm over them, and you should be too."

Her eyes widen. "Oh, I'm not thinking about me. I'm used to her being mean to me. I'm thinking about you, and how she wouldn't accept you because of where, you know... you're from."

I stiffen.

We haven't talked about where I am from since that incident in the lighthouse when Tia tried to make fun of me. If anyone knows how

I felt about that, it is Gaby. She saw my eyes when Tia embarrassed me. She laid her hand on mine and whispered that she didn't care where I was from.

We have never mentioned it again. Not on our daily phonecalls during the school term, not in our texts, not even in our plans to visit each other one day at our own houses. So why is she bringing it up now?

Aaron breaks the awkward silence. "You're the only one who wants her back, Fayson, and we're all confused. Why?"

I sigh, twisting my mouth from side to side. "I told you why. Because everyone deserves a second chance."

I want Tia to come back so Mama will know I did what was right. But also, even though Tia and I don't get along, I know what it's like to have no friends. I don't want her to be alone. Plus Omar, Aaron, Gaby and Ace were her friends before I came along. We are the only

102

kids on this island, apart from a few babies. We should be together.

"Let's just vote and get it over with," Omar groans. "Everyone who wants Tia back, raise your hand."

I raise my hand in the air, but I am the only one.

Omar grins at me smugly. "It's decided then. No more Tia. No talking about Tia, no suggesting Tia comes back. No Tia," he says, swiping his hands in front of him. "It's done. Over. Let's move on."

We decide to head back to Mrs Hammond's house, to accept the case and officially begin the investigation.

Gaby and I walk ahead, with the boys trailing behind. The ground is still damp from all the rain yesterday, but the sun has been out all morning.

The air is cool but smells musky, as it always does after lots of rain.

"Are you mad at me?" Gaby asks, as we follow the road towards Mrs Hammond's house.

My jaw clenches. "Why would I be mad?"

"Well, maybe you're mad because I didn't want Tia back?" she suggests.

I shake my head, pushing my lips together and avoiding her eyes. "Nope. You can do whatever you want," I answer stiffly.

The thing is, I am a little upset. The group voting to not have Tia back was not part of the plan. In my head they would agree with me, and I would call Mama and tell her how wonderful it is here. How we're all getting along, and the island is perfect. "Come and see for yourself," I would tell her, and she would. Mama would pack her bags and take the next boat over.

I take a deep gulp, swallowing the lump in my throat. Now Mama won't come.

We fall silent and I can hear the boys discussing Mrs Hammond and her strange wardrobe and whether her husband is somehow inside it.

"I'll change my vote," Gaby says with a decisive nod. "You're right, we should forgive."

I stare ahead. "You shouldn't change your vote for me. And besides, it wouldn't make a difference. We would still be outnumbered."

She sighs. "I don't want it to affect our friendship. I love you, you're my best friend."

My shoulders drop and I look at her for the first time. I give her a small smile. "I know that, Gaby," I tell her softly. "And I love you too."

Her eyes widen and a broad smile spreads across her face. She slips her arm round my waist, and I slip mine around hers as we turn the curve of the road.

"You're my best friend too, Fayson," she whispers. "And I've never had a best friend before."

I think about Lizzy, and the note. How Lizzy was the bestest friend I ever had. I didn't think anyone would ever come close to her, but now I have Gaby.

Chapter 8

We stand outside Mrs Hammond's gate for the second time today. This time I am the only one desperate to get inside and look for clues.

"Just checking, are we sure we want to do this?" Omar asks nervously. The others don't answer.

"I'm sure," I tell him, pushing the iron gate open and heading up the path alone.

Gaby runs to catch up and links arms with me. "Wherever you go, I go," she says, holding on to me firmly.

"But the dead husband," Omar hisses, as the others follow at a distance.

I knock firmly on the door. "I love a good ghost mystery." I grin. "More for us to investigate!"

Omar shakes his head. "There's something seriously wrong with you."

We wait for Mrs Hammond to open the door, but after a few minutes of waiting, the door remains closed. I knock again. "Could she be out on her walk?"

Gaby shakes her head. "No, she only walks at seven o'clock. It's midday, too early for her evening walk and she has already had her morning one."

We wait in silence. Nothing. I am about to knock again when Gaby turns the handle.

It opens.

"You really need to stop doing that!" I hiss. She widens her eyes innocently. "It's not my fault it was unlocked."

She steps inside the familiar dark living room.

"Mrs Hammond?" Gaby calls out in her cheery voice. "Mrs Hammond, it's me Gaby. Are you there?"

We walk into the centre of the living room and the door slams shut behind us. We jump, spinning round.

Omar, who was the last in, shakes his head frantically. "It wasn't me," he whispers, his eyes wide with terror.

I turn back and look down the hall on the other side of the living room, which leads into the rest of the house. We wait for Mrs Hammond to appear, but she doesn't come. I creep through the living room and down the hall.

The door that leads down to the cellar is on my right. I try the handle, but it's locked, so I continue round the corner, where there is another closed door on the left and a third room at the end of the hall with the door slightly ajar.

"Maybe we should wait in the living room," Gaby whispers nervously.

I glance back at her. "You were the one who opened the door. Don't be scared now."

"I know," she says, trying to keep up with me while tiptoeing. "It's just... I think this is too far."

I ignore her, heading for the room at the end. As I reach the door, I lay my hand on it and close my eyes. I feel a weight on my shoulder and jump, covering my mouth to stifle my scream.

It's Aaron, looking at me weirdly. "What are you doing?" he asks.

I turn back to the door. "In one of my mystery novels, they press their hand on the door to feel if it's warm or cold."

He stares at the door then at me blankly. "What does that prove?"

I shake my head impatiently. "I'm assuming this is the kitchen, from those cupboard doors I can see through the gap. If it's cold, that means no one has been in this room for a while. If it's warm that means someone is in there or has been in there recently." I press my hand on the door again and close my eyes, trying to imagine what could be behind it.

Omar kisses his teeth loudly. "You're talking rubbish," he says irritably.

My head snaps round to glare at him.

He widens his eyes at me defiantly. "You're talking rubbish," he repeats, his voice louder this time. *"If the door is hot, it's on fire,"* he says, mimicking me. *"So we should definitely get out and try not to die, but if it's cold we have travelled to Antarctica, so we need a very, very big coat!"*

Ace chuckles under his breath.

"It makes no sense," he shouts. "Us being here makes no sense. I want to go home. Now."

I spin round to give him a piece of my mind, but stop abruptly and clamp my mouth shut.

"Hello, children." Mrs Hammond's voice echoes down the hallway. "I wasn't expecting you." Gaby rushes forward, spluttering words of apology, the way Gaby does when she is frightened of getting into trouble.

"Mrs Hammond! We knocked, and you didn't answer… and the door was open."

"The door was open?" Mrs Hammond cries, spinning round to look behind her, even though you can't see the front door from where we are.

"Not open, but unlocked," Gaby corrects herself, flapping like a fish out of water. "We didn't mean to walk in, but we thought you may have fallen and no one would know."

That's a lie. But she's good. So good that Mrs Hammond seems to fall for it.

"Well, that is very thoughtful of you," she says. "I was outside hanging out my washing. I can't hear the front door back there."

Omar walks over to the window and peers out into the overgrown backyard. "You hang your washing out there?" he asks.

Mrs Hammond clasps her hands in front of her, There are clothes pegs hooked on to the apron of her dress. "To what do I owe this second visit?"

"I think I know what the knocking is," I blurt out.

Mrs Hammond raises her eyebrows. "You do?"

Aaron slides up next to me. "We do?" he hisses under his breath.

Mrs Hammond takes a step towards us and turns her ear towards me. "Go on."

The others turn to me too, and I avoid their bewildered faces.

I take a breath.

"Don't mess it up," Aaron mutters, without moving his lips.

I glance at the door. All I want is to get in there so we can do our job. If I say the wrong thing, we could lose this case for ever.

"I think it's your husband," I blurt out. "I think he's sending you a very important message." There is silence. I can hear my heart thumping in my chest.

She leans in closer, her eyes glistening. "What's the message?"

I bite my lip, my eyes darting from left to right, my brain ticking fast. I finally settle my eyes on her nervously. "I don't know. That's what we need to find out, and we can only do it if you let us downstairs."

Mrs Hammond's head jerks back and she purses her lips. Her hand slips into her pocket and I can hear the jingle of keys between her fingers. "Well, alright then," she says, pulling a set of keys out of her pocket. "I don't suppose it can do any harm to try."

Aaron pats me on the back, and I feel a squeeze of my arm. I sneak a look at Gaby behind me, and she is beaming.

I watch with baited breath as she slips the old key into the lock and turns it. There is a click. Then she turns the handle and the door creaks open.

Chapter 9

Mrs Hammond waves us towards the open cellar door.

"You know where to find the wardrobe," she says, standing aside.

I glance down the dark wooden staircase, then back at her.

"You not coming, Mrs Hammond?"

She shakes her head. "I never did like it down there. You go ahead and do your investigating." She lays a hand on me as I take the first step. "But if it turns out it is him, you come and find me, you hear? You come and find me straight away."

I nod, avoiding her eyes and the sudden guilt in my stomach. "I will, Mrs Hammond," I mumble.

I take each step carefully, as though the stairs might not hold under me. When I am halfway down, the wall to my right ends and I can see the cellar. It's still dark, still eerie, like in the type of story that keeps me up at night. I reach the bottom of the stairs and stand on the cold stone floor.

I wait until everyone is at the foot of the stairs next to me, before edging towards the wooden wardrobe at the other end of the room.

The five of us stand in a line in front of the wardrobe, staring at it, waiting. As if on cue, the knocking starts, like a slow, rhythmic drum.

Tap... tap... tap.

I listen intently, my heart pounding hard against my chest.

"That's funny..." I wonder aloud. I turn to the others, whose eyes are all fixed on the wardrobe. "Why does the knocking only start when we are in the cellar?"

"Because it's her husband, like you said," Omar hisses impatiently. "You told her that, so maybe that's what it is."

I shake my head, my mind spinning. "So why can't we hear it upstairs?"

They look at me blankly.

"Did you hear the knocking when we entered the house earlier?" I ask. No one responds. "What about when we stood right outside the door, waiting for Mrs Hammond to open it?"

"Maybe we should focus on the knocking we can hear right now," Ace says nervously.

I see the panic etched on their faces. We are never going to make a name for ourselves as a detective agency if we are afraid. I clench my fist and exhale, blowing out all the nervous air I've been holding inside. I stare at the banging wardrobe, rocking back and forth on my feet.

Come on, Fayson. You can do it!

I take a deep breath and march over to the wardrobe, wrapping my hand round the handle. It's now or never.

"No! Fayson, nooo!" they all cry in unison.

I yank the door open.

The knocking stops.

I peer inside. To the left wall. The right wall. The back of the wardrobe.

It is empty, apart from the wooden chest that was here earlier and the same coat hanging up.

I crane my neck upwards, to the top of the wardrobe. Nothing.

I step back and turn to face the others.

"Her husband isn't there. See for yourselves."

One by one, they edge towards the wardrobe, and one by one they take turns looking in.

"See?" I tell them cheerily.

"So what is making that noise?" Ace asks, looking around the room.

"I don't know," I tell him. "But that's why we're here."

"So where do we start?" Aaron asks.

I bite my lip; my mind spinning, my eyes scanning the room. I reach into the wardrobe and run my hand over the coat hanging off the railing. I feel inside the pockets, without a clue of what I am looking for. They're empty.

My eyes fall on the wooden chest.

"Maybe we try to open that."

Everyone's eyes fix on the wooden chest at the back of the wardrobe. We all saw it the first time

Mrs Hammond brought us down here. It was right in front of us when we opened the wardrobe, but for some reason no one thought to open it.

"It's just an empty chest," Omar says, walking around the room "It's probably got her husband's clothes in."

He disappears under the stairs, out of sight.

"Well, we won't know that unless we look," I say firmly.

Omar reappears, pointing behind him. "There's some boxes round here, maybe there are some clues."

I scowl at him. "The sound didn't come from round there, it came from the wardrobe. You know this, Omar."

He rolls his eyes and disappears round the corner again.

I turn to the others. "We can't ignore it. We have to at least look."

Gaby twists her hands in front of her. "This is a lot scarier than I thought it would be."

I reach over to her and lay my hand on her shoulder. "I won't let anything happen to you, Gaby. Okay?"

She smiles weakly.

I let go of her, turn to face the chest then glance over at Aaron. "Can you help me?"

We both reach into the back of the wardrobe. He grabs an iron handle on the left side of the chest, and I grab the other. We lift, and it is surprisingly light as we both manoeuvre the wooden box out of the wardrobe and on to the floor in the middle of the room.

We make a circle round the chest, looking down at it. Omar appears beside his brother, a deep line of worry between his eyebrows.

"It felt empty," Aaron says, breaking the silence.

"It was pretty light," I agree.

Omar's head jerks up, a look of hope in his eyes now. "You think it's empty?" he asks.

I shrug at the same time that Aaron does.

"So... should we open it?" Ace says hesitantly.

No one answers.

I sigh heavily, knowing it's probably going to be me who does it. No one else is volunteering. Slowly, I get down on my knees. I look at the clip between the lid and the body of the case.

Just do it, Fayson!

Before I can talk myself out of it, I quickly unclip the chest and lift the lid, allowing it to fall back. I hold my breath, waiting, but nothing happens.

Aaron is the first to peer in. "It's empty."

The rest of us examine the chest. He's right.

I shake my head, leaning back on my legs. "I don't understand. The sound was definitely coming from the wardrobe, wasn't it?" I look to the others for help.

"Yes," Aaron says. "But just because it made a sound, doesn't mean it is... physical."

"You mean, it could be a ghost?" Ace asks.

"Maybe we should ask Mrs Hammond," Gaby suggests.

"Ask her what?" Omar groans. "She doesn't know, that's why we're here."

Gaby and Omar start to argue.

I raise my hand. "Stop. Can you hear that?"

Everyone falls silent. There it is again. Slowly we all turn our heads to the wardrobe. The door is wide open, the inside completely empty. I can feel my heart pounding against my chest again as I slowly get to my feet.

It is the same slow knock that we heard before, but this time it sounds louder.

"So, it wasn't coming from the chest." Gaby trembles, her hand searching for mine.

No, this time it is obvious where the sound is. It is coming from behind the wardrobe.

Chapter 10

I edge towards the wardrobe, and the others follow close behind. Even Omar has no objections, now it's clear the knocking sound isn't coming from inside.

"How do we get to the sound?" Gaby whispers from behind me.

I stare into the wardrobe, puzzled.

"Maybe move it?" Aaron suggests. "We could try to shift it away from the wall."

We nod.

Gaby, Ace and Omar take one side of the

wardrobe, while Aaron and I take the other. We place our hands firmly on both sides of the wardrobe, gripping it tightly with our fingers.

"On three, we push," Aaron shouts. "One… two… three!"

I lean into the wardrobe, planting my feet firmly into the ground. The wardrobe shifts forward, but only a little. Aaron counts again, and we heave, pushing our bodies into it as hard as we can. The bottom of the wardrobe scrapes against the stone floor. I glance over my shoulder to the back wall. The wardrobe has moved at least a few inches forward, but not enough for any one of us to get around the back.

"Just a little more," I shout.

"Put all your weight into it this time," Aaron says.

"Oh thanks, I was only giving half my energy before," Omar cries sarcastically.

Aaron counts us down and this time I put all my strength into it, so much so that my feet begin to slide backwards. "Keep going," Aaron gasps, through strained breaths. The wardrobe screeches loudly, sliding across the floor. "Okay, okay. Stop!"

I let go, allowing my hands to drop to my sides and taking a deep breath in. When I look up, the wardrobe has moved completely away from the wall. I go around the back and peer behind it and into the darkness.

"What can you see?" Gaby asks.

I squint. There is something, but I can't make out what it is. "I need a light."

I fumble in my pocket for my phone and turn the torch on. It's directed at the ceiling, but as I move it down and my torch lights up the wall, I inhale sharply.

"What? What is it?" Gaby asks.

"There's a door," I whisper.

"No there isn't," Omar says in disbelief.

I step to one side so they can see for themselves. They flash their phone lights behind the wardrobe.

"It's a door!" Gaby cries out.

"No way," Ace gasps.

Aaron shakes his head in shock. "What is this place?"

It is a question we are all beginning to ask. When we first came to Mrs Hammond's house, none of us expected this type of mystery. I stare in wonder at the door blending into the white wall. This could be a scene in any of my detective books! In fact, this is much better.

"Children?" the voice of Mrs Hammond interrupts us from the top of the stairs. "It's time for you to go now."

My shoulders slump. "Please can we stay a bit longer?" I shout up. "We were just getting somewhere."

"No, that will be enough for today," she replies firmly. "It must be time for your lunch.

I'm sure your parents have it all waiting. You can come back tomorrow."

We leave the wardrobe where it is and reluctantly trudge up the wooden steps to where Mrs Hammond is waiting in the hallway.

"We only need a few more minutes," I plead with her, but she will not have it.

"I'm sure you have plans besides hanging around in my basement," she says, closing the cellar door behind us and locking it with the key. She leads us back down the hall and opens the front door, ushering us out.

We step outside.

"So we can come back tomorrow?" I ask earnestly.

"You may return tomorrow at the same time," she says. "Not before, and not after." Mrs Hammond closes the door, leaving us standing on the doorstep.

The sky is dark, as though it's going to rain again. so we quicken our steps, hoping to reach home before it does.

"Why do you think she didn't want us to stay?" Ace asks.

"It's probably time to talk to her husband," Omar mutters.

"I think it's because she likes being on her own," Gaby says. "I don't think she likes people being in her house, not really."

"It's just so weird," I mumble. "We weren't doing anything wrong."

As we follow the road down the small incline, Aaron lets out a small groan. I follow his gaze to see Tia waiting for us in the middle of the road, her arms folded against her chest. I bite my lip nervously. I hope she's not here to upset the others and confirm what they already think about her; that she is mean and not a nice person.

I feel Gaby move to my side, linking arms with me.

"What does she want?" Omar grumbles.

As we approach, Tia steps out in front of me, slowing me down. I stop.

She flashes me a smile. "Are you enjoying taking over my gang?"

I raise an eyebrow, bemused. "We're a detective agency now, not a gang."

"*We're a detective agency now, not a gang,*" she mimics. "You're not a detective agency, you're a bunch of wannabe crime-solvers looking for fake mysteries in lighthouses."

"You're wrong actually," Aaron butts in. "We have an actual case. And you don't have to keep waiting for us at the corner of every

131

road; we get it, you want to come back into the group. But you're not welcome. We voted on it."

I glance at Aaron, and a smile pulls at my lips. I've never seen Aaron like this before. Normally he stays quiet. He never gets involved in arguments, except when his brother taunts him.

Tia must be stunned too, because she doesn't respond.

I walk round her, continuing along the road.

"You really told her," Omar says, patting his brother on the back. It feels like the first time I've seen them agree with each other.

Gaby glances at me. "Still want her to come back?" she asks.

I'm not going to tell her why I want Tia back in the group. "It doesn't matter anyway," I say, glancing up as the sound of thunder echoing in the distance. "We voted, and you guys won. She won't be coming back."

"It's for the best," Gaby says, squeezing my arm. "I know you want to do what's right, but I don't think Tia has changed. In fact, I know for certain she hasn't."

I look at her. "What do you mean?"

We've just reached Gaby's house, and stop outside her front gate.

I nudge her. "Gaby? What has Tia done?"

She lets go of my arm. "What hasn't she done. It's Tia," she says, walking towards her house. "See you tomorrow," she cries, waving her hand in the air.

We wait until she is halfway up her driveway before we continue onwards, along the curve of the road.

"What was that about?" Aaron asks.

I shake my head, baffled. "I don't know."

The sky opens and rain pours down on us. We leave Ace outside his house and run the rest of the way through the pouring rain.

133

We enter the house dripping from head to foot, and a screeching voice comes round the corner.

"No, no! You're getting water everywhere!" Aunty Desiree cries in dismay. "Elma, bring the towels," she shouts down the corridor, before pointing Omar back to the mat by the front door. "Don't you move an inch," she orders us. "Any of you."

We stand on the mat, shivering from our soaking wet clothes, until Elma arrives with towels for each of us. She wraps a towel round me and rubs me down, squeezing the water out of my clothes.

"Oh, you're soaking wet," Elma tuts, wrapping me like a burrito.

I look to Aunty Desiree for permission to move. She nods reluctantly.

"You kids will be the death of me," she cries in despair. "Is it so hard to stay dry for five minutes? Is that too much to ask?"

I waddle through the living room and along the hall to my room. Behind me, I can hear the boys giggling.

"You look like a duck!" Omar cries, laughing hard. "We should have a waddling race." He turns back to the beginning of the hall and Aaron joins him. "Come on, Fayson, don't be boring," he shouts.

I watch them both shuffling to the start of the hall. "Fine," I sigh, waddling back to them, which only sets them off again.

Omar laughs so hard that he loses his balance and topples to the floor. Aaron slides against the wall, tears of laughter streaming down his cheeks.

Chapter 11

I am still laughing when I enter my bedroom ten minutes later. The game of wrapping ourselves tightly in a towel and racing down the hall ended abruptly when Aunty Desiree heard us and shouted from the other end of the house that she hoped we're not still in our wet clothes. So we hobbled to our rooms, giggling.

I close the door behind me with my body and wiggle out of the towel, letting it drop to the floor. I grab some dry clothes out of the built-in wardrobe. I've just finished throwing them on when a glint of white catches my eye over by the glass doors leading outside.

My heart sinks as I notice a white piece of paper pushed between the door and the wall. I walk over, picking it up. Unfolding the note, I scan the page and sure enough it is just what I thought: another message about my secret.

I read the single line over and over, my hand trembling.

WHAT HAPPENED TO LIZZY?

I stare at the message, my heart beating faster and faster. Who is writing these notes? And what do they want from me? Are they going to tell everyone my secret, or do they just want me to suffer?

A sudden knock on the door startles me. Before I can answer, the door opens and Aaron peers in. I quickly fold the note and try to hide it, but it falls from my hand to the floor.

His eyes drop to the piece of paper and for a second neither of us speak. Finally his eyes meet mine and he's looking at me strangely.

"Mum's calling us for lunch," he says before disappearing, leaving the door open.

I stand rooted to the spot, my heart pounding against my chest. Aaron saw the note. Why didn't he mention it? My mind starts scrambling for reasons. Maybe he thought it was rubbish. People have pieces of paper in their hands all the time. There's nothing weird about that.

Suddenly Aaron reappears, and I inhale sharply. He walks into the room. I groan inwardly, wishing I had remembered to lock the door behind me. He stops right in front of me and bends down, picking up the note.

I reach for it but he's too quick.

"Aaron, leave my stuff alone!" I cry, reaching for it again.

He holds it above his head, and with his other hand he reaches into his pocket and pulls out a piece of paper. He takes the two pieces of paper and places them on the bed.

I drop my hand to my side and stare at the two identical notes. Both with the same words written on the outside.

OPEN ME

My mouth falls open as my eyes dart from his note to mine.

"You've been getting them too?" he says, and I feel my whole body let out a gasp of air.

I have no words. My feet are rooted to the ground. This makes no sense. I reach for Aaron's note but he grabs it, closing his fist around it.

"Are you two coming for lunch or what?" Omar shouts from the hall. His irritation changes when he sees us both standing by my bed. He looks from his brother to me, then his eyes move to the bed where our notes lies. He walks in slowly, his eyes not leaving the pieces of paper. He stops across from me and doesn't say a word.

"Omar," I manage to say, through all the feelings swirling around inside me. "Did you get a note too?" I'm barely able to get the words out.

He reaches into his pocket and pulls out a crumpled note. He throws it on the bed and raises his eyes to look at me; they are wide in disbelief.

"Kids! Lunch!" Aunty Desiree shouts down the hall, making us all jump. "I'm not going to call you again; your father only has thirty minutes before he has to take an important call."

Without saying a word, we grab our notes, slip them into our pockets and head towards to the living room.

We sit round the long table filled with mango, chopped bananas, apples and plums, four different juices and six different types of sandwiches. I pick a triangle-shaped chicken sandwich and place it on my plate.

I stare at it as though I have never seen a chicken sandwich before, but my mind is swimming with thoughts about my note, Aaron's note, and now Omar's too.

"You kids okay?" Uncle Edmond asks from the other end of the table. When none of us answer he chuckles, shaking his head. "This is the quietest I've ever seen them."

"We should take a picture," Aunty Desiree agrees. "We'll probably never see this moment again!"

I glance across the table at Omar and Aaron. Neither of them seem able to eat either. Finally Omar pushes his plate away.

"I'm not hungry," he mumbles. "Can I go?"

Aaron pushes his plate to the side too. "I'm not hungry either," he says.

"Me either," I add.

Aunty Desiree and Uncle Edmond look at each other from their opposite ends of the table.

"What's the matter? Are you sick?" Aunty Desiree asks.

We all shake our heads at the same time, but I think maybe we should have said yes, because the uneasy feeling in my stomach is making me feel like I want to throw up.

"Can we go?" Omar asks again, and I'm grateful to him for saying what we all want to say.

Aunty Desiree nods, her brow wrinkled. "Okay, go," she says, waving us away.

Before she can even finish the sentence, we jump to our feet. As I lead the boys along the hall, I can hear Uncle Edmond telling Aunty Desiree how she shouldn't give in to us so easily. But I am barely able to hear her answer, the thunder of my heart in my ears is so loud.

I rush into my room and don't stop until I am by the glass doors. I spin round on my heels as the boys follow me in. Aaron closes the door behind him, and we all stare at each other, stunned.

"So we've all been getting the notes?" I say at last.

Aaron shrugs. "Is it the same?"

"Show me," I say.

Omar shakes his head. "You show yours."

I think about my note and what is written inside. I'm embarrassed to show them. I don't want anyone to know.

"Do you think the others got one too?" Aaron says out loud. I hadn't thought of that. I walk over to my dresser and pick up my phone. I dial Gaby's number and put the phone to my ear.

"Gaby," I say breathlessly down the phone. "I need to ask you a really important question."

"What is it?" she asks. In a rushed gulp of words, I tell her about the notes I have been receiving since we returned to the island. She gasps down the phone. "Fayson, why didn't you tell me?"

I lean against the dresser, glancing over at the twins, who are watching me intently.

"I was afraid," I admit. "But why I really called was to ask if you had received any notes…?"

There is a pause. The boys come over to where I am and lean in to listen.

"Well, yes," she admits. "I was too afraid to tell anyone."

I let out a gasp of air.

The boys nudge me. "What did she say?" Omar asks. I give them a nod.

When I put down the phone, I am filled with a mixture of emotions.

"Shall I call Ace?" Aaron asks, and he leaves the room before I can answer.

Omar and I wait in silence, him cross-legged on the floor, me pacing the room biting my nails. A few minutes later Aaron returns. He throws his phone on the bed.

"He's been getting letters too." He sighs. "And he's not been doing good because of it."

I slump on to the bed. "Time to call another meeting."

Back in the hut, for the second time that day, I feel especially nervous. More nervous than I felt the first day I came here; when all eyes were on me and I wanted so much to be part of the group.

The truth is, I don't know how to talk about the note without revealing my secret, but there seems no other way. Now that I know we have all received notes, I can't ignore it any more. I have to do the one thing I have been avoiding.

I need to tell them my secret.

It is the only way to get to the bottom of this.

Chapter 12

"Shall I start?" I say nervously, looking at each of them.

My chest is tied in knots and my hands are sweaty. Omar stares at his fingers intently, picking at his nails. Aaron can't seem to hold my gaze and Ace can't keep still, looking everywhere but at me. Even Gaby can't look me in the eye.

"After I got to my room, I saw the note." My hands tremble as I open the note. I turn it around to show them what it says.

WHAT HAPPENED TO LIZZY?

The blood drains from my face and my skin tingles with embarrassment.

"You don't have to explain to us," Gaby says. She looks to the others for support, and they all agree. "We shouldn't be forced to talk about things that are personal," she continues. "Especially when we know who is behind it."

I fold the note into my pocket.

I didn't want to believe it was Tia. I hoped she had changed, and she would eventually return to the group. But it's the only answer that makes sense. Everyone has received a note, except for Tia. She's gone too far this time.

"What are we going to do about it?" Aaron says.

"We're going to confront her," Ace says firmly. His eyes are fiery. "She's not going to get away with this." He stops abruptly, sinking back into the beanbag.

"I agree with Ace," Omar says, wrapping his hands round his legs and leaning back. "We have to confront her."

"Is that what we all think?" I ask, looking around.

They all nod their heads adamantly, so we leave the hut and head to Tia's house.

When we reach Tia's, I knock on the huge oak door that towers above us. Minutes later the door opens and Olivia their maid smiles out at us.

"Is Tia in?" I ask. She nods, leading us inside. I haven't been here since the summer party and it seems weird to see it so empty. We take the winding staircase and turn left on the first floor. Then along a long corridor until we reach a white door on the left.

The maid knocks.

"Come in," calls a voice from inside, and Olivia lets us into Tia's bedroom. She is sitting on her window seat with a book in her hand.

"Ms Tia, you have visitors."

Tia looks up from her book. She raises her eyebrows when she sees us. The maid leaves, closing the door behind her.

This is exactly how I expected Tia's bedroom to be. Large enough to fit two of my bedrooms back home. There is a huge double bed against the wall by the door. The bed is filled with pink and white cushions and enough pillows for five houses. The wooden floor is covered by a fluffy white mat. Her white walls are covered with photos of her doing lots of sports, and medals hanging off every photograph. Sometimes two medals on one photo. There is a white desk against the far wall, next to a large closet.

"What are you doing here?" she demands, spinning round and folding her legs under her. I feel Gaby's arm in mine.

"We've got you," she whispers, squeezing my arm.

I step forward and take a deep breath. Knowing Tia, she is not going to like what I'm about to say. She could laugh and deny it, she could get mad and kick us out of her house. She might even complain to the adults. There is no way of knowing how this is going to go and that makes me nervous.

"We know you've been sending us letters," Ace blurts out, before I can say a word.

Tia looks at us blankly.

"Don't act like you don't know what we're talking about," he says angrily. "It's not cool what you've done. You're trying to ruin our lives, and it's messed up. You're messed up."

A flicker of hurt crosses Tia's face. She closes the book and places it beside her. She clasps her hands together. "I don't know what you're talking about."

Ace scoffs. "You're lying! You know exactly what we're talking about, because you did it." He points at her angrily. "It's always you because… because you never want us to be happy. You never want us to do anything without you."

Ace looks at Aaron, his best friend in the group, and his face is earnest. "I can't do this," he tells him. "I can't listen to her lies." He storms off and we hear his feet running down the stairs.

"I'll go check on him," Aaron says, leaving the room.

Tia's eyes widen and a small smirk pulls at her lips. "What's wrong with Ace?"

"Maybe he doesn't like people threatening to tell his secrets," I suggest dryly.

She looks at me blankly. "I don't know what you're talking about."

Omar groans, throwing his hands up in the air. "I knew it. I knew she would say that."

He sits his hands on his hips, like his dad does when he's about to tell us off for being too noisy, or me for not saying my words right. "This is why we can't be friends, Tia," he says, shaking his head. "And I liked you."

My head jerks back and he catches my confused face.

"Well, I did!" he says. "She never bothered me, not really, but this is out of order, Tia, this is too much."

I stare at him. "Why? Because now it affects you?"

Omar shrugs, his expression very matter-of-fact. "Well, yeah."

I roll my eyes and turn back to Tia, who is watching us bemused.

"Just tell us why you did it," I say tiredly.

Tia raises her hands either side of her. "Did what? I still don't know what any of you are talking about. You've all said a lot of nothing."

I pull out the note from my pocket and wave it in her face. "This. The notes. The threats to tell everyone our secrets. You know what you did, Tia. Just tell us why, and how you know these secrets about us."

Tia stares at the piece of paper in my hand. "Can I read it?"

Gaby grabs my arm, shaking her head. "No, Fayson, that's what she wants."

I pull away from Gaby. "What does it matter? She already knows. She wrote it."

I hand Tia the note and she stares at it for some time. Then she looks up at me. "I didn't write this."

Gaby snatches the note and hands it back to me. "Come on, Fayson. She's not going to admit it."

Gaby and Omar storm out of the room, but I stay. I stare right into Tia's eyes, trying to figure out how someone could be so mean.

"It doesn't matter what you know about Lizzy," I tell her, my voice breaking. "She was my friend."

As I turn to follow the others, Tia calls after me. "Fayson, I didn't write that."

I stop at the door and turn to look at her. Her eyes are blurry with tears.

"I swear to you, I didn't write it," she says. "I don't know who Lizzy is... I don't know how to contact Lizzy. I don't even know where she lives... You can believe me or not believe me. It's the truth."

I turn on my heel and leave, but this doesn't feel right. Something feels off.

Could Tia actually be telling the truth? She seems genuine.

I know she was awful to all of us in the past, but this time I believe her.

The others are waiting for me outside Tia's front door. Ace is pacing back and forth.

"Well?" Aaron asks as I approach. "What did she say? Did she admit it?"

I stare off into the distance. I dig my hand into my pocket and feel the note there.

"She said she didn't do it," I tell them. The group implodes with indignation.

"Of course she did," Gaby says, throwing her hands up in the air.

"So what now?" Ace says, inhaling deeply.

My mind is whizzing, and I can barely focus with all their questions.

"Let's go home," I tell them. "Tomorrow we meet at Mrs Hammond's to continue the investigation."

We head down the driveway, towards the road.

"I must admit, that Mrs Hammond case is getting kind of exciting," Omar says.

His brother pats him on the shoulder. "You not scared any more?"

"I didn't say that," Omar jokes, making the boys laugh. "But I'm more excited than scared. I mean, who would have thought there was a door behind that old, stinky wardrobe?"

They fall into lively discussions about what could be behind the door, but I am barely listening.

Gaby nudges me. "Aren't you glad we didn't vote Tia back into the group?" she asks.

I don't answer, because my head is full of questions.

Later that evening, I am lying in bed, my arms under my head, staring at the ceiling and willing it to give me some answers. I thought when we confronted Tia I would get all the answers I needed and that would be the end of it. Instead, I have come away with more questions.

I didn't want to tell the group, but the way Tia talked made me believe her. She wasn't being the usual arrogant Tia. Her eyes were earnest, almost pleading to be believed. The others didn't seem to notice this, but I did. I saw a side of Tia I have never seen before. She didn't have her guard up; she wasn't ready to argue like always.

I believed she didn't write the notes.

But if not her, then who?

Chapter 13

Early the next morning, we all stand outside Mrs Hammond's house. I'm surprised we all made it in time.

Gaby gives the door a knock and we wait.

"I'm not going to lie," Omar says, tilting back and forth on his heels. "I was excited to come here today."

"Me too," Ace replies, just as the door opens. Mrs Hammond beams out at us.

"Aah," she says. "You came!" And she ushers us in.

Mrs Hammond leads us down the familiar hall until we reach the door on the right, then we wait as she unlocks it.

This time, we rush down the stairs, pushing each other out the way to get there first. Down in the cellar, the old wardrobe is pulled away from the wall, where we left it.

Omar shines his phone light on the wall behind. "There!"

I squeeze between the wardrobe and the wall, and push the hidden door. It doesn't budge.

"Look for a handle," Gaby suggests.

"Or a latch to pull," Aaron chimes in.

"So, a handle then…" Omar rolls his eyes at his brother.

Ace joins me and we both search the door for anything that will help us get to the other side.

"A keyhole," Ace announces, his eyes bright with excitement.

Omar shines his light where Ace is pointing and sure enough there is a keyhole, but no key.

We all set about looking for a key. We search the door, the wardrobe, the floor. Even the wooden chest.

"How about the keys upstairs, on Mrs Hammond's key ring?" Omar suggests to me.

So we go to find Mrs Hammond while the others continue to look in the cellar.

"It might be the one or it might not," Omar says, talking non-stop. "Either way it's worth a try, you know?"

I smile to myself. It is hard to believe this is the same Omar who didn't want to step inside this house yesterday.

As we reach the top of the stairs, I check the door for the key, in case Mrs Hammond forgot to take it with her, but it's not there. We glance into the living room, looking for her, but it's empty.

"Mrs Hammond," I call out. "Mrs Hammond, are you there?"

The house is silent, but I know she's here. She would never leave us alone in her house.

"Which way?" Omar asks, rapidly pointing left, then right.

I point down the hall towards the kitchen. "I remember there was another door on the left…" We reach the door and I knock. No one answers. I turn the handle slowly. "Mrs Hammond?"

I push the door back and peer into a dark bedroom with a small iron bed in the middle. The walls are painted dark green with white flowers, and she has sheets to match. The curtains are drawn as though it's night-time and someone is asleep, but there is no one in the room.

Even though I can see it is empty, I call out to Mrs Hammond once more.

Omar peers over my shoulder, scanning the room using the light on his phone. He nudges me and points over to an old beechwood dressing table.

Hanging off the mirror attached to the dressing table are a set of keys.

"You keep watch," I whisper to Omar. He nods, looking up and down the hall while I slip into her room. I tiptoe across the old wooden floor. Every floorboard creaks under my weight, and each time it creaks, I freeze, waiting for Mrs Hammond to appear.

Finally, after much stopping and starting, I reach the dressing table. I pull the set of keys down and it moves a photograph that had been slid into the corner of the mirror. With the set of keys in one hand, I replace the photo with my other.

It's a small black and white photo, and in the photo is a young man, around twenty, maybe twenty-one. He has on a hat tilted to the side, and he's wearing a short-sleeved white shirt, with loose trousers and dark shoes. He has his arm draped around a woman with short curled hair, wearing a knee-length skirt and a pale blouse.

I squint at the photo. It must be Mrs Hammond and her husband, when they were much younger. I smile.

"Come on," Omar hisses.

I straighten the photo and rush out, closing the door behind me. We tiptoe down the hall and run down the stairs to where the others are still trying to find the key.

I jingle the keys in my hand to get their attention.

We rush over to the wall and, with someone holding a light over me, I go through the five keys on the key ring. The first one doesn't turn it, neither does the second. The third one is the wrong size, a small silver key that is much too small, but I try it anyway.

I tuck the third key into the palm of my hand, along with the others that don't work. The excitement has died down, and when the fourth key doesn't open it, there is a collective groan among us.

"What if none of those keys work," Omar moans.

I ignore him. It has to be this one, or we'll have to start the search all over again. I push the key into the lock and turn it.

There is a click, and we gasp. I push the door inwards and it opens.

Omar, Ace, Gaby and Aaron rush me, throwing their arms round me and hugging me tightly. We jump up and down, chanting:

"DI ISLAND CREW!

DI ISLAND CREW!

DI ISLAND CREW!"

When we have finished celebrating, we rush through the door to see what is on the other side.

We enter a long narrow tunnel. I wave my phone light along the wall. It's filled with drawings. Pictures of the ocean with a boat lying on the shore. We form a line: me in front, then Omar, because he argued that he found the key too so he should go second. Gaby begrudgingly stands behind him. Behind her is Ace, and at the back is Aaron. The ceiling is low but gives us enough room to stand, except Ace, who is forced to tilt his head to avoid banging it.

With all our phone lights held out in front of us, we follow the tunnel. The drawings continue.

The tunnel comes to an abrupt stop. A stone wall. We all flicker our lights around, looking for a way out.

"Is this it?" Omar cries in dismay. I search underneath our feet, then shine the light above us.

"Look," I shout, getting their attention. Everyone looks up, and there is a trapdoor above us. I flash the light around it: another keyhole.

As I fidget with the keys, the knocking starts again, from just above our heads.

"The noise has been coming from upstairs the entire time?" Gaby hisses in a lowered tone.

I slip the first key in the lock, and it turns immediately. There is a hushed cheer between us and Omar gives me a pat on the back.

I raise my hands above my head, placing both palms on the trapdoor, and push. It falls back with a bang.

I peer up through the hole. I can see a room with a lightbulb on the ceiling.

The banging is loud now, as though it is right in front of us.

Knock, knock, knock…

I reach into the opening and place both my hands on either side, using my arms to pull myself through the gap. I sit on the edge, my legs still dangling down, and look around the room.

My mouth falls open.

"What is it?" Omar cries from the tunnel below.

Slowly, I pull myself up to standing and stare at what is in front of me in disbelief.

Omar pulls himself through, then Gaby, Ace next, then Aaron. And as each of them steps into the room, their mouths fall open, just like mine. It is only when Aaron enters that the person across from us speaks.

"Hello, children," Mrs Hammond says. She is sitting on a wooden chair, facing us. "Did you enjoy that little adventure?"

We're in a small kitchen that is painted dark green. There is a stove against the wall to the right of the trapdoor, and a door that must lead outside.

In front of us, Mrs Hammond sits at a round table. On the table next to her is a recording device with a familiar sound coming from it, a recording:

Knock

Knock

Knock.

To the left of the table is an open door that leads down the hall of the house.

"Oh, don't look so shocked," she says, laughing. It's the first time I've seen Mrs Hammond laugh. Her eyes light up and it is contagious. Omar and Ace giggle, even though they don't know what is happening.

"Sit down," she says, pointing to the table next to her, which is covered with a flowery plastic cloth. There is a jug of water with five glasses and a pineapple upside-down cake. We all take a seat around the table, and she pours us each a glass of water. Then she slowly cuts the pineapple cake and hands us each a slice on a plate.

I lock eyes with Gaby.

What is going on? Gaby mouths.

I shrug slightly, without catching Mrs Hammond's attention. When she has fixed us all a slice of cake, she sits back down on her hard wooden chair.

"My husband would be the happiest man in the world if he was here to see this," she says, chuckling again. Her shoulders bounce with every laugh. "You did it exactly how he expected. Maybe the clues were a little too easy, but it was never meant to be hard, just lots of fun. He wanted it to be fun."

My forehead wrinkles as my brain ticks, trying to understand what is happening. "Your husband planned all that?" I ask slowly, as the pieces fall into place.

Mrs Hammond nods and her eyes light up again. "It was meant to be for our children.

We were going to adopt a little girl. Sonia, her name was. She was six years old, and the fourth child we had tried to adopt. But just like all the others, it fell through at the last minute.

"She was given to another family, but it was never fully explained to us why, only that it was a tough choice." She sighs, her smile fading. "It was too late by then. My husband had built it. The hidden door, the tunnel, the trapdoor; it was all for them. All of them. But they never came."

She jumps to her feet and starts busying herself, closing the trapdoor and locking it while still talking.

My heart sinks at how much Mrs Hammond wanted children but never got them. I feel Gaby take my hand and she has tears in her eyes.

"'There will be other children to enjoy it,' he said. 'It won't go to waste.'

"'Which kids?' I said to him, we live on a tiny island. 'There's no one here but us.' Then the families came, but by then he had gone."

We all fall silent. This no longer feels like a victory. My heart is heavy for Mrs Hammond and I can tell by the way the others have lowered their eyes to the ground that they feel the same.

She turns to face us, smiling. "And now here you are, keeping his memory alive. It was all he ever wanted; all I ever wanted."

I clear my throat. "So when Gaby came to the door telling you about us solving cases…"

She nods, before filling in the blanks. "I thought, 'This is just what they need, and this is what Edgar,' my husband, 'would have wanted'."

I sink back into the chair, as if the breath has been knocked out of me.

Mrs Hammond clatters around the kitchen, moving a few plates and cups from the sink to the cupboard above her, the recording machine still playing.

Aaron reaches across the table and stops it, with a heavy sigh. "Guess we don't need that any more," he says sombrely.

We are quiet when we leave Mrs Hammond's house. Even her cheery goodbye isn't enough to shake the feeling of sadness we all feel for her.

"She tricked us," Ace says quietly, in disbelief.

"And all the time, she had planned it all," Omar mumbles, kicking stones with his feet.

A small laugh escapes me. "Remember the first day she showed us the cellar? She was so serious, I really believed her."

The mood begins to change as Omar imitates Mrs Hammond, pretending to find his keys in his pocket, then slowly taking them out with an exaggerated raise of one eyebrow. "Follow me," he says in a screeching voice, pretending to go down imaginary stairs.

"It's kind of nice, though, don't you think?" Gaby says. "She trusted us with her husband's secret project. That must mean she liked us?"

"Well I like her," Omar says, shrugging. "She seems like she would be a good mum."

I nod, feeling a lump in my throat. "I think she would be the best mum," I agree.

We are so busy talking that we don't see the figure waiting for us outside the agency hut until we are almost in front of her.

Tia leans against the hut, her legs crossed at the ankle. The mood drops suddenly. She gives us a short wave.

"Hey, besties," she says, flashing us a smile. She leans off the hut. "After much consideration, I've decided I won't be accused of something I didn't do. And since you couldn't find out the truth, I did it for you."

She flashes us a sarcastic smile. My heart is thumping against my chest. "You know who wrote the notes?" I whisper.

Chapter 14

Gaby frowns at me.

"Fayson, you don't believe her, do you?" she asks.

I take a deep breath, knowing that siding with Tia would not go down well with the crew. What Tia has to say could break up Di Island Crew. It could ruin our friendships.

I take a second to gather myself, running my hand across my face. Finally I lock eyes with Gaby.

"Can we at least hear her out?"

The others reluctantly enter the hut, but Gaby turns to face me. "This isn't fair," she cries. "We voted her out. She shouldn't be allowed in here. And honestly, Fayson, you made me feel terrible for not supporting you with the vote, but now you're not supporting me."

I stare at her, bewildered. "I didn't tell you how to vote, Gaby."

"No, not in words," she says breathlessly, "but it's how you made me feel. You made me feel like my friendship was only good enough if I agreed with you." She fumbles for the right words. "That if I did exactly what you wanted, I would be a good friend. And now... now you won't even do the same for me."

I stare at her in dismay, my heart sinking.

"Are you coming?" Tia calls out to us.

Gaby turns to walk in, but I take her hand.

"Gaby," I say, feeling sick inside. "I'm sorry. I was hurt, and I did want you to agree with me, but you were right to stick to your vote. I'm learning what it is to be a friend, a real friend, and I'm not very good at it yet. You are my first real friend. I want you to tell me when I get it wrong."

She sniffs back tears, nodding her head.

"It's okay for us to want different things," I tell her. "We'll always be friends, even when we disagree."

"No matter what happens?" she asks.

I wrap my arms around her and hug her tightly. "No matter what happens, I love you."

I slip my hand into hers and we enter the hut together, where everyone is waiting.

Tia turns to me, completely ignoring the glares she's getting from the boys. "Finally!" she says. "Can I stand at the front? Am I allowed?"

"No, you're not," Ace snaps.

I turn to everyone. "Let's just hear what Tia has to say." I give Gaby's hand a reassuring squeeze.

"So," Tia says, clasping her hands together. I can't help but admire how confident she is. Despite the group hating her and throwing her daggers, she doesn't flinch.

"Do you remember when you barged into my room yesterday and accused me of writing threatening letters?"

"We didn't say 'threatening letters'," Gaby speaks up, but she sinks back as soon as Tia's eyes fall on her.

"Well," Tia says. "I don't know what the rest of your notes said, but I did read Fayson's, and I don't even know who Lizzy is."

"You would say that," Ace shoots back at her. "You're not going to admit it, are you?"

I listen as they go back and forth, nervously biting my nail, which I haven't done since I was seven. If Tia doesn't say something soon to prove her innocence, this could all backfire on me. The others will blame me for allowing her into the hut. For believing her.

"Okay," Tia says nodding her head. "What was the point of the letters? Threatening to tell your secret? So why don't you tell the group your secrets?"

Everyone looks around the group nervously. "What?" Ace mumbles.

"She's right," I tell them. "I've been thinking about this as well. 'How can I take the power away from the person holding my secret?' I knew straight away the answer was to tell you guys, but I was scared of what you would think of me."

"I thought she knew who the person was?" Gaby says, nodding at Tia.

I lay my hand on her shoulder firmly. "It doesn't matter who did it. We need to put a stop to it." I nod at the boys in the far corner of the room. "We're supposed to be friends. We should know each other's secrets. We should be able to say anything in this room and it stays in this room; between us."

"No!" Gaby shouts. She looks at me with frightened eyes. "I don't want you to tell them your secret, Fayson," she blurts out. "I didn't mean for it to go this far, honestly I didn't."

She spins round to face Ace, who is staring at her, confused. "I don't want you to tell them either, Ace. That was between you and me. I don't want anyone else to know, please believe me."

Ace steps away from the wall, his mouth falling open. "You?"

Gaby fidgets with her hands nervously, her eyes fluttering from me to the boys.

"I didn't want Tia to come back to our group," she explains. "I thought if I pretended she wrote the letters then she would be banned for ever. The group is perfect right now, we laugh so much. No one is scared to speak or say what they think. If Tia comes back, all that will change. I know you said it wouldn't, Fayson, but you don't know her like I do. It would go back to the way it was, and I hated it then."

"I knew it," I respond. "There's no way Tia could have known about my secret. Only two people knew. You and Mama. I didn't think it could be you until we confronted Tia. She said something that didn't make sense. She said she wouldn't know how to contact Lizzy, that she didn't even know where Lizzy lived… and it all fell into place."

"I don't get it," Omar says, stroking his head.

I sigh, knowing if we are going to be honest with each other, then I have to start. I should be the first one.

"Lizzy isn't real." My face flushes as I say the words out loud. "She's fake. I made her up. I've never had a real best friend. Lizzy was imaginary."

Silence falls around the room and I wrap my arms round myself, lowering my eyes to the floor and hoping it will open up and swallow me.

"My dad is having money troubles," Ace says. "He's been having them for a while. We might have to sell this house, so I don't know if I'll be back. This might be my last time on Lighthouse Island."

I raise my eyes to look at him, but he hangs his head. Aaron reaches across and grabs his arm. It's all that Ace needs. He turns to Aaron and sinks his head into his shoulders. We all rush over and wrap our arms round him.

I glance over to Tia, who is standing awkwardly by the desk. I beckon her over but she shakes her head, shuddering. "I feel for Ace, but I don't do that," she says, pointing to our group hug.

I don't know how long we hold Ace. It doesn't matter. What matters is how close I feel to them in that moment. When we finally let go, there are tears in all our eyes.

"If you're selling your house, can I have your bike?" Omar asks. Ace chuckles.

"Can I have your beanie collection?" Aaron teases.

"No, I'm taking that with me," Ace snaps, pushing Aaron away. "Anyway, you haven't told us your secret yet. You trying to get away with it?"

All eyes turn to the twins. They both glance at each other, then at me.

"My letter said that the only reason we wanted Fayson to come to the island was because our parents forced us," Aaron says quietly.

Omar nods. "Mine said the same. It said that we didn't really like Fayson."

I blush, though I'm not really surprised. "That's not a secret. I know you don't like me."

"It's not true, though," Omar says. "Maybe at the beginning I thought you wouldn't fit in… but I actually like having a sister."

I raise my eyebrows. "I'm your sister now?"

Omar rolls his eyes. "Whatever."

"What about you, Gaby?" Tia asks. "Did you write yourself a note?"

Gaby reaches into the small bag across her shoulder and pulls out a note. We all move over to her to read it. She cringes. "I'm sorry."

I read the note over her shoulder.

I KNOW WHAT YOU DID TO THE GROUP.

"What did you do to the group?" Omar asks, puzzled.

We all look at him.

"Ohhhh," he says as it clicks. "Okay, phew." He walks away, wiping pretend sweat off his face.

"So I have a suggestion," I say loudly to get their attention. "One, we put Gaby's weird threatening letters down to making a bad mistake. Her intentions were to protect the group, she just went about it the wrong way. Right?"

The group nod in agreement. I move over to Tia.

"Same thing with Tia. I think we give her a second chance, because people make mistakes, right?"

Silence falls among the group.

"We can't have one rule for one of us and another rule for someone else," I tell them firmly. "It has to be fair. This should be a group where we can be honest with each other, where we can keep each other's secrets, and where we are fair to everyone."

I look around the room.

"I say we vote for Tia again, Gaby."

We send Tia out of the hut so we can vote. Five minutes later I call her in.

She walks into the room and for the first time Tia seems nervous. Her hands fidget by her sides as she walks to the front. I stand next to her and turn to the group.

"So, who wants to tell her?"

*

The next day all six of us walk to Mrs Hammond's house, our arms full. Tia has brought flowers picked from her garden. Gaby has a jug of her mother's favourite carrot juice. I am carrying a picnic basket filled with biscuits and cakes that Elma baked, while the boys are carrying plates and a set of foldable chairs and table.

Gaby knocks on the front door, and within seconds it opens. Mrs Hammond beams out at us.

"Well, what a surprise!" she cries. "What is all this?"

"We've come to spend the afternoon with you, Mrs Hammond," I tell her, smiling.

Her eyes widen with delight. I point to her front garden.

"Would you like to join us outside for a picnic?"

She clasps her hands to her face and steps out as the boys and Tia set up the chairs and foldable table. Gaby and I escort Mrs Hammond into her front yard and sit her down on one of the chairs.

Tia gives her the flowers and Aaron fills her plate with cakes and biscuits. We sit down around her.

"You'd better get used to this, Mrs Hammond," I tell her. "We'll be coming here every week in the holidays."

She squeezes my hand. "You know," she whispers. "You have made my day, children, yes you have."

"That's what we do, Mrs Hammond," Gaby says, beaming. "We're the best detective agency in the whole wide world. We can fix anything, even your day."

And as they talk amongst themselves, my phone buzzes. It's Mama!

How is it going?

It's going great, I text back. *Tia is back in Di Island Crew, and we solved another mystery. We're sitting in Mrs Hammond's front garden having a picnic. She gave us a mystery to solve.*

I pause, then add: *It so peaceful here, Mama. You would love it.*

I stare at my phone, heart in my mouth as I wait for her to reply. I see the dots flashing as she types. Then it stops. I sigh, slumping down into the grass. Maybe Mama will never want to come here. Maybe I should stop trying to convince her.

My phone pings as a message comes through.

It sounds wonderful there. Maybe I might like it after all.

I clutch the phone to my chest, smiling widely. Finally, there's a chance I could get what I have always wanted!

Mama on Lighthouse Island.

Next time,
Di Island Crew investigates...

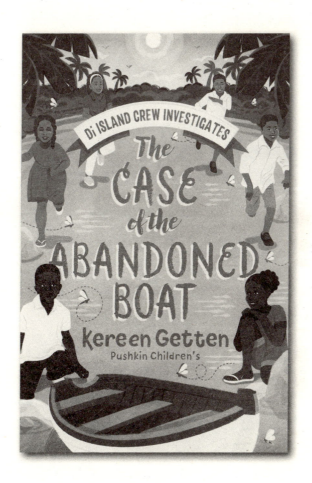

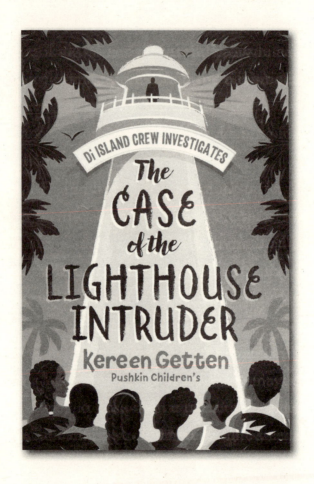

The first book in the Di Island Crew Investigates
series, *The Case of the Lighthouse Intruder*, was a
Waterstones Book of the Month.